YOUTH AND
THE BRIGHT MEDUSA

———

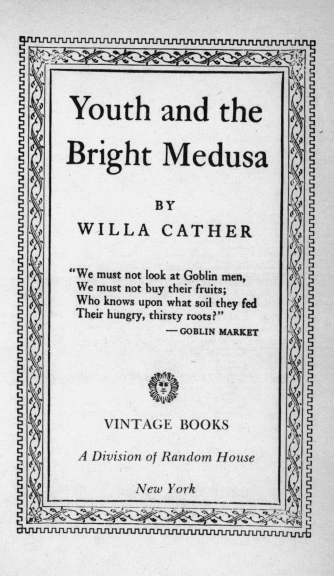

Youth and the Bright Medusa

BY

WILLA CATHER

"We must not look at Goblin men,
We must not buy their fruits;
Who knows upon what soil they fed
Their hungry, thirsty roots?"
— GOBLIN MARKET

VINTAGE BOOKS

A Division of Random House

New York

FIRST VINTAGE BOOKS EDITION, September 1975
Copyright 1920 by Willa Cather.
Renewal copyright 1948 by the Executors of the Estate
of Willa Cather.
All rights reserved under International and Pan-American
Copyright Conventions. Published in the United States by
Random House, Inc., New York, and simultaneously in
Canada by Random House of Canada Limited, Toronto.
Originally published by Alfred A. Knopf, Inc., in 1920.

Library of Congress Cataloging in Publication Data
Cather, Willa Sibert, 1873–1947.
  Youth and the bright Medusa.
  CONTENTS: Coming, Aphrodite!—The diamond mine.—
A gold slipper. [etc.]
  I. Title.
PZ3.C2858Yo12 [PS3505.A87]   813'.5'2   75–11560
ISBN 0–394–71684–1

Manufactured in the United States of America

The author wishes to thank *McClure's Magazine*, *The Century Magazine* and *Harper's Magazine* for their courtesy in permitting the re-publication of three stories in this collection.

The last four stories in the volume, *Paul's Case*, *A Wagner Matinée*, *The Sculptor's Funeral*, "*A Death in the Desert*," are re-printed from the author's first book of stories, entitled "The Troll Garden," published in 1905.

CONTENTS

COMING, APHRODITE!

COMING, APHRODITE!

I

Don Hedger had lived for four years on the top floor of an old house on the south side of Washington Square, and nobody had ever disturbed him. He occupied one big room with no outside exposure except on the north, where he had built in a many-paned studio window that looked upon a court and upon the roofs and walls of other buildings. His room was very cheerless, since he never got a ray of direct sunlight; the south corners were always in shadow. In one of the corners was a clothes closet, built against the partition, in another a wide divan, serving as a seat by day and a bed by night. In the front corner, the one farther from the window, was a sink, and a table with two gas burners where he sometimes cooked his food. There, too, in the perpetual dusk, was the dog's bed, and often a bone or two for his comfort.

The dog was a Boston bull terrier, and Hedger explained his surly disposition by the fact that he had been bred to the point where it told on his nerves. His name was Caesar III, and he had taken prizes at very exclusive dog shows. When he and his master went out to prowl about University Place or to promenade along West Street, Caesar III was invariably fresh and shining. His pink skin showed through his mottled coat, which glistened as if it had just been rubbed with olive oil, and he wore a brass-studded collar, bought at the smartest saddler's. Hedger, as often as not, was hunched up in an old striped blanket coat, with a shapeless felt hat pulled over his bushy hair, wearing black shoes that had become grey, or brown ones that had become black, and he never put on gloves unless the day was biting cold.

Early in May, Hedger learned that he was to have a new neighbour in the rear apartment—two rooms, one large and one small, that faced the west. His studio was shut off from the larger of these rooms by double doors, which, though they were fairly tight, left him a good deal at the mercy of the occupant. The rooms had been leased, long before he came there, by a trained nurse who considered herself knowing in old furniture. She went to auction sales and bought up mahogany and dirty brass and stored it away here, where she meant to live when she retired from nursing. Meanwhile, she sub-let her rooms, with their precious furniture, to young people who came to New York to "write" or to "paint"—who proposed to live by the sweat of the brow rather than of the hand, and who desired artistic surroundings. When Hedger first moved in, these rooms were occupied by a young man who tried to write plays,—and who kept on trying until a week ago, when the nurse had put him out for unpaid rent.

A few days after the playwright left, Hedger heard an ominous murmur of voices through the bolted double doors: the lady-like intonation of the nurse—doubtless exhibiting her treasures—and another voice, also a woman's, but very different; young, fresh, unguarded, confident. All the same, it would be very annoying to have a woman in there. The only bath-room on the floor was at the top of the stairs in the front hall, and he would always be running into her as he came or went from his bath. He would have to be more careful to see that Caesar didn't leave bones about the hall, too; and she might object when he cooked steak and onions on his gas burner.

As soon as the talking ceased and the women left, he forgot them. He was absorbed in a study of paradise fish at the Aquarium, staring out at people through the glass and green water of their tank. It was a highly gratifying idea; the incommunicability of one stratum of animal life with another,—though Hedger pretended it was only an experiment in unusual lighting. When he heard trunks knocking against the sides of the narrow hall, then he realized that she was moving in at once. Toward noon, groans and deep gasps and the creaking of ropes, made

5

him aware that a piano was arriving. After the tramp of the movers died away down the stairs, somebody touched off a few scales and chords on the instrument, and then there was peace. Presently he heard her lock her door and go down the hall humming something; going out to lunch, probably. He stuck his brushes in a can of turpentine and put on his hat, not stopping to wash his hands. Caesar was smelling along the crack under the bolted doors; his bony tail stuck out hard as a hickory withe, and the hair was standing up about his elegant collar.

Hedger encouraged him. "Come along, Caesar. You'll soon get used to a new smell."

In the hall stood an enormous trunk, behind the ladder that led to the roof, just opposite Hedger's door. The dog flew at it with a growl of hurt amazement. They went down three flights of stairs and out into the brilliant May afternoon.

Behind the Square, Hedger and his dog descended into a basement oyster house where there were no tablecloths on the tables and no handles on the coffee cups, and the floor was covered with sawdust, and Caesar was always welcome,—not that he needed any such precautionary flooring. All the carpets of Persia would have been safe for him. Hedger ordered steak and onions absentmindedly, not realizing why he had an apprehension that this dish might be less readily at hand hereafter. While he ate, Caesar sat beside his chair, gravely disturbing the sawdust with his tail.

6

After lunch Hedger strolled about the Square for the dog's health and watched the stages pull out;—that was almost the very last summer of the old horse stages on Fifth Avenue. The fountain had but lately begun operations for the season and was throwing up a mist of rainbow water which now and then blew south and sprayed a bunch of Italian babies that were being supported on the outer rim by older, very little older, brothers and sisters. Plump robins were hopping about on the soil; the grass was newly cut and blindingly green. Looking up the Avenue through the Arch, one could see the young poplars with their bright, sticky leaves, and the Brevoort glistening in its spring coat of paint, and shining horses and carriages,—occasionally an automobile, mis-shapen and sullen, like an ugly threat in a stream of things that were bright and beautiful and alive.

While Caesar and his master were standing by the fountain, a girl approached them, crossing the Square. Hedger noticed her because she wore a lavender cloth suit and carried in her arms a big bunch of fresh lilacs. He saw that she was young and handsome,—beautiful, in fact, with a splendid figure and good action. She, too, paused by the fountain and looked back through the Arch up the Avenue. She smiled rather patronizingly as she looked, and at the same time seemed delighted. Her slowly curving upper lip and half-closed eyes seemed to say: "You're gay, you're exciting, you are quite the right sort of thing; but you're none too fine for me!"

7

In the moment she tarried, Caesar stealthily approached her and sniffed at the hem of her lavender skirt, then, when she went south like an arrow, he ran back to his master and lifted a face full of emotion and alarm, his lower lip twitching under his sharp white teeth and his hazel eyes pointed with a very definite discovery. He stood thus, motionless, while Hedger watched the lavender girl go up the steps and through the door of the house in which he lived.

"You're right, my boy, it's she! She might be worse looking, you know."

When they mounted to the studio, the new lodger's door, at the back of the hall, was a little ajar, and Hedger caught the warm perfume of lilacs just brought in out of the sun. He was used to the musty smell of the old hall carpet. (The nurse-lessee had once knocked at his studio door and complained that Caesar must be somewhat responsible for the particular flavour of that mustiness, and Hedger had never spoken to her since.) He was used to the old smell, and he preferred it to that of the lilacs, and so did his companion, whose nose was so much more discriminating. Hedger shut his door vehemently, and fell to work.

Most young men who dwell in obscure studios in New York have had a beginning, come out of something, have somewhere a home town, a family, a paternal roof. But Don Hedger had no such background. He was a foundling, and had grown up in a school for homeless boys,

COMING, APHRODITE!

where book-learning was a negligible part of the curriculum. When he was sixteen, a Catholic priest took him to Greensburg, Pennsylvania, to keep house for him. The priest did something to fill in the large gaps in the boy's education,—taught him to like "Don Quixote" and "The Golden Legend," and encouraged him to mess with paints and crayons in his room up under the slope of the mansard. When Don wanted to go to New York to study at the Art League, the priest got him a night job as packer in one of the big department stores. Since then, Hedger had taken care of himself; that was his only responsibility. He was singularly unencumbered; had no family duties, no social ties, no obligations toward any one but his landlord. Since he travelled light, he had travelled rather far. He had got over a good deal of the earth's surface, in spite of the fact that he never in his life had more than three hundred dollars ahead at any one time, and he had already outlived a succession of convictions and revelations about his art.

Though he was not but twenty-six years old, he had twice been on the verge of becoming a marketable product; once through some studies of New York streets he did for a magazine, and once through a collection of pastels he brought home from New Mexico, which Remington, then at the height of his popularity, happened to see, and generously tried to push. But on both occasions Hedger decided that this was something he didn't wish to carry further,—simply the old thing over again and got nowhere,—so he took enquiring dealers experiments in a "later manner," that made them put him out of the shop. When he ran short of money, he could always get any amount of commercial work; he was an expert draughtsman and worked with lightning speed. The rest of his time he spent in groping his way from one kind of painting into another, or travelling about without luggage, like a tramp, and he was chiefly occupied with getting rid of ideas he had once thought very fine.

Hedger's circumstances, since he had moved to Washington Square, were affluent compared to anything he had ever known before. He was now able to pay advance rent and turn the key on his studio when he went away for four months at a stretch. It didn't occur to him to wish to be richer than this. To be sure, he did without a great many things other people think necessary, but he didn't miss them, because he had never had them. He belonged to no clubs, visited no houses, had no studio friends, and he ate his dinner alone in some decent little restaurant, even on Christmas and New Year's. For days together he talked to nobody but his dog and the janitress and the lame oysterman.

After he shut the door and settled down to his paradise fish on that first Tuesday in May, Hedger forgot all about his new neighbour. When the light failed, he took Caesar out for a walk. On the way home he did his marketing on West Houston Street, with a one-eyed Italian woman who always cheated him. After he had cooked his beans and scallopini, and drunk half a bottle of Chianti, he put his dishes in the sink and went up on the roof to smoke. He was the only person in the house who ever went to the roof, and he had a secret understanding with the janitress about it. He was to have "the privilege of the roof," as she said, if he opened the heavy trapdoor on sunny days to air out the upper hall, and was watchful to close it when rain threatened. Mrs. Foley was fat and dirty and hated to climb stairs,—besides, the roof was reached by a perpendicular iron ladder, definitely inaccessible to a woman of her bulk, and the iron door at the top of it was too heavy for any but Hedger's strong arm to lift. Hedger was not above medium height, but he practised with weights and dumb-bells, and in the shoulders he was as strong as a gorilla.

So Hedger had the roof to himself. He and Caesar often slept up there on hot nights, rolled in blankets he had brought home from Arizona. He mounted with Caesar under his left arm. The dog had never learned to climb a perpendicular ladder, and never did he feel so much his master's greatness and his own dependence upon him, as when he crept under his arm for this perilous ascent. Up there was even gravel to scratch in, and a dog could do whatever he liked, so long as he did not bark. It was a kind of Heaven, which no one was strong enough to reach but his great, paint-smelling master.

On this blue May night there was a slender, girlish

looking young moon in the west, playing with a whole company of silver stars. Now and then one of them darted away from the group and shot off into the gauzy blue with a soft little trail of light, like laughter. Hedger and his dog were delighted when a star did this. They were quite lost in watching the glittering game, when they were suddenly diverted by a sound,—not from the stars, though it was music. It was not the Prologue to Pagliacci, which rose ever and anon on hot evenings from an Italian tenement on Thompson Street, with the gasps of the corpulent baritone who got behind it; nor was it the hurdy-gurdy man, who often played at the corner in the balmy twilight. No, this was a woman's voice, singing the tempestuous, over-lapping phrases of Signor Puccini, then comparatively new in the world, but already so popular that even Hedger recognized his unmistakable gusts of breath. He looked about over the roofs; all was blue and still, with the well-built chimneys that were never used now standing up dark and mournful. He moved softly toward the yellow quadrangle where the gas from the hall shone up through the half-lifted trap-door. Oh yes! It came up through the hole like a strong draught, a big, beautiful voice, and it sounded rather like a professional's. A piano had arrived in the morning, Hedger remembered. This might be a very great nuisance. It would be pleasant enough to listen to, if you could turn it on and off as you wished; but you couldn't. Caesar, with the gas light shining on his collar and his ugly but sensitive face, panted and looked up for information. Hedger put down a reassuring hand.

"I don't know. We can't tell yet. It may not be so bad."

He stayed on the roof until all was still below, and finally descended, with quite a new feeling about his neighbour. Her voice, like her figure, inspired respect, —if one did not choose to call it admiration. Her door was shut, the transom was dark; nothing remained of her but the obtrusive trunk, unrightfully taking up room in the narrow hall.

II

For two days Hedger didn't see her. He was painting eight hours a day just then, and only went out to hunt for food. He noticed that she practised scales and exercises for about an hour in the morning; then she locked her door, went humming down the hall, and left him in peace. He heard her getting her coffee ready at about the same time he got his. Earlier still, she passed his room on her way to her bath. In the evening she sometimes sang, but on the whole she didn't bother him. When he was working well he did not notice anything much. The morning paper lay before his door until he reached out for his milk bottle, then he kicked the sheet inside and it lay on the floor until evening. Sometimes he read it and sometimes he did not. He forgot there was anything of importance going on in the world outside of his third floor studio. Nobody had ever taught him that he ought to be interested in other people; in the Pittsburgh steel strike, in the Fresh Air Fund, in the scandal about the Babies' Hospital. A grey wolf, living in a Wyoming canyon, would hardly have been less concerned about these things than was Don Hedger.

One morning he was coming out of the bath-room at the front end of the hall, having just given Caesar his bath and rubbed him into a glow with a heavy towel. Before the door, lying in wait for him, as it were, stood a tall figure in a flowing blue silk dressing gown that fell away from her marble arms. In her hands she carried various accessories of the bath.

"I wish," she said distinctly, standing in his way, "I wish you wouldn't wash your dog in the tub. I never heard of such a thing! I've found his hair in the tub, and I've smelled a doggy smell, and now I've caught you at it. It's an outrage!"

Hedger was badly frightened. She was so tall and positive, and was fairly blazing with beauty and anger. He stood blinking, holding on to his sponge and dog-soap, feeling that he ought to bow very low to her. But what he actually said was:

"Nobody has ever objected before. I always wash the tub,—and, anyhow, he's cleaner than most people."

"Cleaner than me?" her eyebrows went up, her white arms and neck and her fragrant person seemed to scream at him like a band of outraged nymphs. Something flashed through his mind about a man who was turned into a dog, or was pursued by dogs, because he unwittingly intruded upon the bath of beauty.

"No, I didn't mean that," he muttered, turning scarlet under the bluish stubble of his muscular jaws. "But I know he's cleaner than I am."

"That I don't doubt!" Her voice sounded like a soft shivering of crystal, and with a smile of pity she drew the folds of her voluminous blue robe close about her and allowed the wretched man to pass. Even Caesar was frightened; he darted like a streak down the hall, through the door and to his own bed in the corner among the bones.

Hedger stood still in the doorway, listening to indignant sniffs and coughs and a great swishing of water about the sides of the tub. He had washed it; but as he had washed it with Caesar's sponge, it was quite possible that a few bristles remained; the dog was shedding now. The playwright had never objected, nor had the jovial illustrator who occupied the front apartment,—but he, as he admitted, "was usually pye-eyed, when he wasn't in Buffalo." He went home to Buffalo sometimes to rest his nerves.

It had never occurred to Hedger that any one would mind using the tub after Caesar;—but then, he had never seen a beautiful girl caparisoned for the bath before. As soon as he beheld her standing there, he realized the unfitness of it. For that matter, she ought not to step into a tub that any other mortal had bathed in; the illustrator was sloppy and left cigarette ends on the moulding.

All morning as he worked he was gnawed by a spiteful desire to get back at her. It rankled that he had been so vanquished by her disdain. When he heard her locking her door to go out for lunch, he stepped quickly into the hall in his messy painting coat, and addressed her.

"I don't wish to be exigent, Miss,"—he had certain grand words that he used upon occasion—"but if this is your trunk, it's rather in the way here."

"Oh, very well!" she exclaimed carelessly, dropping her keys into her handbag. "I'll have it moved when I can get a man to do it," and she went down the hall with her free, roving stride.

Her name, Hedger discovered from her letters, which the postman left on the table in the lower hall, was Eden Bower.

III

In the closet that was built against the partition separating his room from Miss Bower's, Hedger kept all his wearing apparel, some of it on hooks and hangers, some of it on the floor. When he opened his closet door now-a-days, little dust-coloured insects flew out on downy wing, and he suspected that a brood of moths were hatching in his winter overcoat. Mrs. Foley, the janitress, told him to bring down all his heavy clothes and she would give them a beating and hang them in the court.

The closet was in such disorder that he shunned the encounter, but one hot afternoon he set himself to the task. First he threw out a pile of forgotten laundry and tied it up in a sheet. The bundle stood as high as his middle when he had knotted the corners. Then he got his shoes and overshoes together. When he took his overcoat from its place against the partition, a long ray of yellow light shot across the dark enclosure,—a knot hole, evidently, in the high wainscoating of the west room. He had never noticed it before, and without realizing what he was doing, he stooped and squinted through it.

Yonder, in a pool of sunlight, stood his new neighbour, wholly unclad, doing exercises of some sort before a long gilt mirror. Hedger did not happen to think how unpardonable it was of him to watch her. Nudity was not improper to any one who had worked so much from the figure, and he continued to look, simply because he had never seen a woman's body so beautiful as this one,— positively glorious in action. As she swung her arms and changed from one pivot of motion to another, muscular energy seemed to flow through her from her toes to her finger-tips. The soft flush of exercise and the gold of afternoon sun played over her flesh together, enveloped her in a luminous mist which, as she turned and twisted, made now an arm, now a shoulder, now a thigh, dissolve in pure light and instantly recover its outline with the next gesture. Hedger's fingers curved as if he were holding a crayon; mentally he was doing the whole figure in a single running line, and the charcoal seemed to explode in his hand at the point where the energy of each gesture was discharged into the whirling disc of light, from a foot or shoulder, from the up-thrust chin or the lifted breasts.

He could not have told whether he watched her for six minutes or sixteen. When her gymnastics were over, she paused to catch up a lock of hair that had come down, and examined with solicitude a little reddish mole that grew under her left arm-pit. Then, with her hand on her hip, she walked unconcernedly across the room and disappeared through the door into her bedchamber.

Disappeared—Don Hedger was crouching on his knees, staring at the golden shower which poured in through the west windows, at the lake of gold sleeping on the faded Turkish carpet. The spot was enchanted; a vision out of Alexandria, out of the remote pagan past, had bathed itself there in Helianthine fire.

When he crawled out of his closet, he stood blinking at the grey sheet stuffed with laundry, not knowing what had happened to him. He felt a little sick as he contemplated the bundle. Everything here was different; he hated the disorder of the place, the grey prison light, his old shoes and himself and all his slovenly habits. The black calico curtains that ran on wires over his big window were white with dust. There were three greasy frying pans in the sink, and the sink itself— He felt desperate. He couldn't stand this another minute. He took up an armful of winter clothes and ran down four flights into the basement.

"Mrs. Foley," he began, "I want my room cleaned this afternoon, thoroughly cleaned. Can you get a woman for me right away?"

"Is it company you're having?" the fat, dirty janitress enquired. Mrs. Foley was the widow of a useful Tammany man, and she owned real estate in Flatbush. She was huge and soft as a feather bed. Her face and arms were permanently coated with dust, grained like wood where the sweat had trickled.

"Yes, company. That's it."

"Well, this is a queer time of the day to be asking for a cleaning woman. It's likely I can get you old Lizzie, if she's not drunk. I'll send Willy round to see."

Willy, the son of fourteen, roused from the stupor and stain of his fifth box of cigarettes by the gleam of a quarter, went out. In five minutes he returned with old Lizzie, —she smelling strong of spirits and wearing several jackets which she had put on one over the other, and a number of skirts, long and short, which made her resemble an animated dish-clout. She had, of course, to borrow her equipment from Mrs. Foley, and toiled up the long flights, dragging mop and pail and broom. She told Hedger to be of good cheer, for he had got the right woman for the job, and showed him a great leather strap she wore about her wrist to prevent dislocation of tendons. She swished about the place, scattering dust and splashing soapsuds, while he watched her in nervous despair. He stood over Lizzie and made her scour the sink, directing her roughly, then paid her and got rid of her. Shutting the door on his failure, he hurried off with his dog to lose himself among the stevedores and dock labourers on West Street.

A strange chapter began for Don Hedger. Day after day, at that hour in the afternoon, the hour before his neighbour dressed for dinner, he crouched down in his closet to watch her go through her mysterious exercises. It did not occur to him that his conduct was detestable; there was nothing shy or retreating about this unclad girl,—a bold body, studying itself quite coolly and evidently well pleased with itself, doing all this for a purpose. Hedger scarcely regarded his action as conduct at all; it was something that had happened to him. More than once he went out and tried to stay away for the whole afternoon, but at about five o'clock he was sure to find himself among his old shoes in the dark. The pull of that aperture was stronger than his will,—and he had always considered his will the strongest thing about him. When she threw herself upon the divan and lay resting, he still stared, holding his breath. His nerves were so on edge that a sudden noise made him start and brought out the sweat on his forehead. The dog would come and tug at his sleeve, knowing that something was wrong with his master. If he attempted a mournful whine, those strong hands closed about his throat.

When Hedger came slinking out of his closet, he sat down on the edge of the couch, sat for hours without moving. He was not painting at all now. This thing, whatever it was, drank him up as ideas had sometimes done, and he sank into a stupor of idleness as deep and dark as the stupor of work. He could not understand it; he was no boy, he had worked from models for years, and a woman's body was no mystery to him. Yet now he did nothing but sit and think about one. He slept very little, and with the first light of morning he awoke as completely possessed by this woman as if he had been with her all the night before. The unconscious operations of life went on in him only to perpetuate this excitement. His brain held but one image now—vibrated, burned with it. It was a heathenish feeling; without friendliness, almost without tenderness.

Women had come and gone in Hedger's life. Not having had a mother to begin with, his relations with them, whether amorous or friendly, had been casual. He got on well with janitresses and wash-women, with Indians and with the peasant women of foreign countries. He had friends among the silk-skirt factory girls who came to eat their lunch in Washington Square, and he sometimes took a model for a day in the country. He felt an unreasoning antipathy toward the well-dressed women he saw coming out of big shops, or driving in the Park. If, on his way to the Art Museum, he noticed a pretty girl standing on the steps of one of the houses on upper

Fifth Avenue, he frowned at her and went by with his shoulders hunched up as if he were cold. He had never known such girls, or heard them talk, or seen the inside of the houses in which they lived; but he believed them all to be artificial and, in an aesthetic sense, perverted. He saw them enslaved by desire of merchandise and manufactured articles, effective only in making life complicated and insincere and in embroidering it with ugly and meaningless trivialities. They were enough, he thought, to make one almost forget woman as she existed in art, in thought, and in the universe.

He had no desire to know the woman who had, for the time at least, so broken up his life,—no curiosity about her every-day personality. He shunned any revelation of it, and he listened for Miss Bower's coming and going, not to encounter, but to avoid her. He wished that the girl who wore shirt-waists and got letters from Chicago would keep out of his way, that she did not exist. With her he had naught to make. But in a room full of sun, before an old mirror, on a little enchanted rug of sleeping colours, he had seen a woman who emerged naked through a door, and disappeared naked. He thought of that body as never having been clad, or as having worn the stuffs and dyes of all the centuries but his own. And for him she had no geographical associations; unless with Crete, or Alexandria, or Veronese's Venice. She was the immortal conception, the perennial theme.

The first break in Hedger's lethargy occurred one after-

out to dine. They went into her music room, laughed and
talked for a few minutes, and then took her away with
them. They were gone a long while, but he did not go
out for food himself; he waited for them to come back.
At last he heard them coming down the hall, gayer and
more talkative than when they left. One of them sat down
at the piano, and they all began to sing. This Hedger
found absolutely unendurable. He snatched up his hat
and went running down the stairs. Caesar leaped beside
him, hoping that old times were coming back. They had
supper in the oysterman's basement and then sat down in
front of their own doorway. The moon stood full over
the Square, a thing of regal glory; but Hedger did not
see the moon; he was looking, murderously, for men.
Presently two, wearing straw hats and white trousers and
carrying canes, came down the steps from his house. He
rose and dogged them across the Square. They were
laughing and seemed very much elated about something.
As one stopped to light a cigarette, Hedger caught from
the other:

"Don't you think she has a beautiful talent?"

His companion threw away his match. "She has a
beautiful figure." They both ran to catch the stage.

Hedger went back to his studio. The light was shining
from her transom. For the first time he violated her
privacy at night, and peered through that fatal aperture.
She was sitting, fully dressed, in the window, smoking a

cigarette and looking out over the housetops. He watched her until she rose, looked about her with a disdainful, crafty smile, and turned out the light.

The next morning, when Miss Bower went out, Hedger followed her. Her white skirt gleamed ahead of him as she sauntered about the Square. She sat down behind the Garibaldi statue and opened a music book she carried. She turned the leaves carelessly, and several times glanced in his direction. He was on the point of going over to her, when she rose quickly and looked up at the sky. A flock of pigeons had risen from somewhere in the crowded Italian quarter to the south, and were wheeling rapidly up through the morning air, soaring and dropping, scattering and coming together, now grey, now white as silver, as they caught or intercepted the sunlight. She put up her hand to shade her eyes and followed them with a kind of defiant delight in her face.

Hedger came and stood beside her. "You've surely seen them before?"

"Oh, yes," she replied, still looking up. "I see them every day from my windows. They always come home about five o'clock. Where do they live?"

"I don't know. Probably some Italian raises them for the market. They were here long before I came, and I've been here four years."

"In that same gloomy room? Why didn't you take mine when it was vacant?"

"It isn't gloomy. That's the best light for painting."

"Oh, is it? I don't know anything about painting. I'd like to see your pictures sometime. You have such a lot in there. Don't they get dusty, piled up against the wall like that?"

"Not very. I'd be glad to show them to you. Is your name really Eden Bower? I've seen your letters on the table."

"Well, it's the name I'm going to sing under. My father's name is Bowers, but my friend Mr. Jones, a Chicago newspaper man who writes about music, told me to drop the 's.' He's crazy about my voice."

Miss Bower didn't usually tell the whole story,—about anything. Her first name, when she lived in Huntington, Illinois, was Edna, but Mr. Jones had persuaded her to change it to one which he felt would be worthy of her future. She was quick to take suggestions, though she told him she "didn't see what was the matter with 'Edna.'"

She explained to Hedger that she was going to Paris to study. She was waiting in New York for Chicago friends who were to take her over, but who had been detained. "Did you study in Paris?" she asked.

"No, I've never been in Paris. But I was in the south of France all last summer, studying with C——. He's the biggest man among the moderns,—at least I think so."

Miss Bower sat down and made room for him on the bench. "Do tell me about it. I expected to be there by this time, and I can't wait to find out what it's like."

Hedger began to relate how he had seen some of this Frenchman's work in an exhibition, and deciding at once that this was the man for him, he had taken a boat for Marseilles the next week, going over steerage. He proceeded at once to the little town on the coast where his painter lived, and presented himself. The man never took pupils, but because Hedger had come so far, he let him stay. Hedger lived at the master's house and every day they went out together to paint, sometimes on the blazing rocks down by the sea. They wrapped themselves in light woollen blankets and didn't feel the heat. Being there and working with C—— was being in Paradise, Hedger concluded; he learned more in three months than in all his life before.

Eden Bower laughed. "You're a funny fellow. Didn't you do anything but work? Are the women very beautiful? Did you have awfully good things to eat and drink?"

Hedger said some of the women were fine looking, especially one girl who went about selling fish and lobsters. About the food there was nothing remarkable,— except the ripe figs, he liked those. They drank sour wine, and used goat-butter, which was strong and full of hair, as it was churned in a goat skin.

"But don't they have parties or banquets? Aren't there any fine hotels down there?"

"Yes, but they are all closed in summer, and the country people are poor. It's a beautiful country, though."

"How, beautiful?" she persisted.

"If you want to go in, I'll show you some sketches, and you'll see."

Miss Bower rose. "All right. I won't go to my fencing lesson this morning. Do you fence? Here comes your dog. You can't move but he's after you. He always makes a face at me when I meet him in the hall, and shows his nasty little teeth as if he wanted to bite me."

In the studio Hedger got out his sketches, but to Miss Bower, whose favourite pictures were Christ Before Pilate and a redhaired Magdalen of Henner, these landscapes were not at all beautiful, and they gave her no idea of any country whatsoever. She was careful not to commit herself, however. Her vocal teacher had already convinced her that she had a great deal to learn about many things.

"Why don't we go out to lunch somewhere?" Hedger asked, and began to dust his fingers with a handkerchief —which he got out of sight as swiftly as possible.

"All right, the Brevoort," she said carelessly. "I think that's a good place, and they have good wine. I don't care for cocktails."

Hedger felt his chin uneasily. "I'm afraid I haven't shaved this morning. If you could wait for me in the Square? It won't take me ten minutes."

Left alone, he found a clean collar and handkerchief, brushed his coat and blacked his shoes, and last of all dug up ten dollars from the bottom of an old copper kettle he had brought from Spain. His winter hat was of such a complexion that the Brevoort hall boy winked at the porter as he took it and placed in on the rack in a row of fresh straw ones.

IV

That afternoon Eden Bower was lying on the couch in her music room, her face turned to the window, watching the pigeons. Reclining thus she could see none of the neighbouring roofs, only the sky itself and the birds that crossed and recrossed her field of vision, white as scraps of paper blowing in the wind. She was thinking that she was young and handsome and had had a good lunch, that a very easy-going, light-hearted city lay in the streets below her; and she was wondering why she found this queer painter chap, with his lean, bluish cheeks and heavy black eyebrows, more interesting than the smart young men she met at her teacher's studio.

Eden Bower was, at twenty, very much the same person that we all know her to be at forty, except that she knew a great deal less. But one thing she knew: that she was to be Eden Bower. She was like some one standing before a great show window full of beautiful and costly things, deciding which she will order. She understands that they will not all be delivered immediately, but one by one they will arrive at her door. She already knew some of the many things that were to happen to her; for instance, that the Chicago millionaire who was going to take her abroad with his sister as chaperone, would eventually press his claim in quite another manner. He was the most circum-spect of bachelors, afraid of everything obvious, even of women who were too flagrantly handsome. He was a nervous collector of pictures and furniture, a nervous patron of music, and a nervous host; very cautious about his health, and about any course of conduct that might make him ridiculous. But she knew that he would at last throw all his precautions to the winds.

People like Eden Bower are inexplicable. Her father sold farming machinery in Huntington, Illinois, and she had grown up with no acquaintances or experiences out-side of that prairie town. Yet from her earliest childhood she had not one conviction or opinion in common with the people about her,—the only people she knew. Before she was out of short dresses she had made up her mind that she was going to be an actress, that she would live far away in great cities, that she would be much admired by men and would have everything she wanted. When she was thirteen, and was already singing and reciting for church entertainments, she read in some illustrated maga-zine a long article about the late Czar of Russia, then just come to the throne or about to come to it. After that, lying in the hammock on the front porch on summer evenings, or sitting through a long sermon in the family pew, she amused herself by trying to make up her mind whether she would or would not be the Czar's mistress when she played in his Capital. Now Edna had met this fascinating word only in the novels of Ouida,—her hard-worked little mother kept a long row of them in the up-stairs storeroom, behind the linen chest. In Huntington, women who bore that relation to men were called by a very different name, and their lot was not an enviable one; of all the shabby and poor, they were the shabbiest. But then, Edna had never lived in Huntington, not even before she began to find books like "Sapho" and "Mademoiselle de Maupin," secretly sold in paper covers throughout Illinois. It was as if she had come into Huntington, into the Bowers family, on one of the trains that puffed over the marshes behind their back fence all day long, and was waiting for another train to take her out.

As she grew older and handsomer, she had many beaux, but these small-town boys didn't interest her. If a lad kissed her when he brought her home from a dance, she was indulgent and she rather liked it. But if he pressed her further, she slipped away from him, laughing. After she began to sing in Chicago, she was consistently discreet. She stayed as a guest in rich people's houses, and she knew that she was being watched like a rabbit in a laboratory. Covered up in bed, with the lights out, she thought her own thoughts, and laughed.

This summer in New York was her first taste of freedom. The Chicago capitalist, after all his arrangements were made for sailing, had been compelled to go to Mexico to look after oil interests. His sister knew an excellent singing master in New York. Why should not a discreet, well-balanced girl like Miss Bower spend the summer there, studying quietly? The capitalist suggested that his sister might enjoy a summer on Long Island; he would rent the Griffith's place for her, with all the servants, and Eden could stay there. But his sister met this proposal with a cold stare. So it fell out, that between selfishness and greed, Eden got a summer all her own,—which really did a great deal toward making her an artist and whatever else she was afterward to become. She had time to look about, to watch without being watched; to select diamonds in one window and furs in another, to select shoulders and moustaches in the big hotels where she went to lunch. She had the easy freedom of obscurity and the consciousness of power. She enjoyed both. She was in no hurry.

While Eden Bower watched the pigeons, Don Hedger sat on the other side of the bolted doors, looking into a pool of dark turpentine, at his idle brushes, wondering why a woman could do this to him. He, too, was sure of his future and knew that he was a chosen man. He could not know, of course, that he was merely the first to fall under a fascination which was to be disastrous to a few men and pleasantly stimulating to many thousands. Each of these two young people sensed the future, but not completely. Don Hedger knew that nothing much would ever happen to him. Eden Bower understood that to her a great deal would happen. But she did not guess that her neighbour would have more tempestuous adventures sitting in his dark studio than she would find in all the capitals of Europe, or in all the latitude of conduct she was prepared to permit herself.

V

One Sunday morning Eden was crossing the Square with a spruce young man in a white flannel suit and a panama hat. They had been breakfasting at the Brevoort and he was coaxing her to let him come up to her rooms and sing for an hour.

"No, I've got to write letters. You must run along now. I see a friend of mine over there, and I want to ask him about something before I go up."

"That fellow with the dog? Where did you pick him up?" the young man glanced toward the seat under a sycamore where Hedger was reading the morning paper.

"Oh, he's an old friend from the West," said Eden easily. "I won't introduce you, because he doesn't like people. He's a recluse. Good-bye. I can't be sure about Tuesday. I'll go with you if I have time after my lesson." She nodded, left him, and went over to the seat littered with newspapers. The young man went up the Avenue without looking back.

"Well, what are you going to do today? Shampoo this animal all morning?" Eden enquired teasingly.

Hedger made room for her on the seat. "No, at twelve o'clock I'm going out to Coney Island. One of my models is going up in a balloon this afternoon. I've often promised to go and see her, and now I'm going."

Eden asked if models usually did such stunts. No, Hedger told her, but Molly Welch added to her earnings in that way. "I believe," he added, "she likes the excitement of it. She's got a good deal of spirit. That's why I like to paint her. So many models have flaccid bodies."

"And she hasn't, eh? Is she the one who comes to see you? I can't help hearing her, she talks so loud."

"Yes, she has a rough voice, but she's a fine girl. I don't suppose you'd be interested in going?"

"I don't know," Eden sat tracing patterns on the asphalt with the end of her parasol. "Is it any fun? I got up feeling I'd like to do something different today. It's the first Sunday I've not had to sing in church. I had that engagement for breakfast at the Brevoort, but it wasn't very exciting. That chap can't talk about anything but himself."

Hedger warmed a little. "If you've never been to Coney Island, you ought to go. It's nice to see all the people; tailors and bar-tenders and prize-fighters with their best girls, and all sorts of folks taking a holiday."

Eden looked sidewise at him. So one ought to be interested in people of that kind, ought one? He was certainly a funny fellow. Yet he was never, somehow, tiresome. She had seen a good deal of him lately, but she kept wanting to know him better, to find out what made him different from men like the one she had just left—whether

33

he really was as different as he seemed. "I'll go with you," she said at last, "if you'll leave that at home." She pointed to Caesar's flickering ears with her sunshade.

"But he's half the fun. You'd like to hear him bark at the waves when they come in."

"No, I wouldn't. He's jealous and disagreeable if he sees you talking to any one else. Look at him now."

"Of course, if you make a face at him. He knows what that means, and he makes a worse face. He likes Molly Welch, and she'll be disappointed if I don't bring him."

Eden said decidedly that he couldn't take both of them. So at twelve o'clock when she and Hedger got on the boat at Desbrosses street, Caesar was lying on his pallet, with a bone.

Eden enjoyed the boat-ride. It was the first time she had been on the water, and she felt as if she were embarking for France. The light warm breeze and the plunge of the waves made her very wide awake, and she liked crowds of any kind. They went to the balcony of a big, noisy restaurant and had a shore dinner, with tall steins of beer. Hedger had got a big advance from his advertising firm since he first lunched with Miss Bower ten days ago, and he was ready for anything.

After dinner they went to the tent behind the bathing beach, where the tops of two balloons bulged out over the canvas. A red-faced man in a linen suit stood in front of the tent, shouting in a hoarse voice and telling the people that if the crowd was good for five dollars more, a beautiful young woman would risk her life for their entertainment. Four little boys in dirty red uniforms ran about taking contributions in their pill-box hats. One of the balloons was bobbing up and down in its tether and people were shoving forward to get nearer the tent.

"Is it dangerous, as he pretends?" Eden asked.

"Molly says it's simple enough if nothing goes wrong with the balloon. Then it would be all over, I suppose."

"Wouldn't you like to go up with her?"

"I? Of course not. I'm not fond of taking foolish risks."

Eden sniffed. "I shouldn't think sensible risks would be very much fun."

Hedger did not answer, for just then every one began to shove the other way and shout, "Look out. There she goes!" and a band of six pieces commenced playing furiously.

As the balloon rose from its tent enclosure, they saw a girl in green tights standing in the basket, holding carelessly to one of the ropes with one hand and with the other waving to the spectators. A long rope trailed behind to keep the balloon from blowing out to sea.

As it soared, the figure in green tights in the basket diminished to a mere spot, and the balloon itself, in the brilliant light, looked like a big silver-grey bat, with its wings folded. When it began to sink, the girl stepped through the hole in the basket to a trapeze that hung below, and gracefully descended through the air, holding to the rod with both hands, keeping her body taut and her feet close together. The crowd, which had grown very large by this time, cheered vociferously. The men took off their hats and waved, little boys shouted, and fat old women, shining with the heat and a beer lunch, murmured admiring comments upon the balloonist's figure. "Beautiful legs, she has!"

"That's so," Hedger whispered. "Not many girls would look well in that position." Then, for some reason, he blushed a slow, dark, painful crimson.

The balloon descended slowly, a little way from the tent, and the red-faced man in the linen suit caught Molly Welch before her feet touched the ground, and pulled her to one side. The band struck up "Blue Bell" by way of welcome, and one of the sweaty pages ran forward and presented the balloonist with a large bouquet of artificial flowers. She smiled and thanked him, and ran back across the sand to the tent.

"Can't we go inside and see her?" Eden asked. "You can explain to the door man. I want to meet her." Edging forward, she herself addressed the man in the linen suit and slipped something from her purse into his hand.

They found Molly seated before a trunk that had a mirror in the lid and a "make-up" outfit spread upon the tray. She was wiping the cold cream and powder from her neck with a discarded chemise.

"Hello, Don," she said cordially. "Brought a friend?" Eden liked her. She had an easy, friendly manner, and

36

there was something boyish and devil-may-care about her.

"Yes, it's fun. I'm mad about it," she said in reply to Eden's questions. "I always want to let go, when I come down on the bar. You don't feel your weight at all, as you would on a stationary trapeze."

The big drum boomed outside, and the publicity man began shouting to newly arrived boatloads. Miss Welch took a last pull at her cigarette. "Now you'll have to get out, Don. I change for the next act. This time I go up in a black evening dress, and lose the skirt in the basket before I start down."

"Yes, go along," said Eden. "Wait for me outside the door. I'll stay and help her dress."

Hedger waited and waited, while women of every build bumped into him and begged his pardon, and the red pages ran about holding out their caps for coins, and the people ate and perspired and shifted parasols against the sun. When the band began to play a two-step, all the bathers ran up out of the surf to watch the ascent. The second balloon bumped and rose, and the crowd began shouting to the girl in a black evening dress who stood leaning against the ropes and smiling. "It's a new girl," they called. "It ain't the Countess this time. You're a peach, girlie!"

The balloonist acknowledged these compliments, bowing and looking down over the sea of upturned faces,—but Hedger was determined she should not see him, and he darted behind the tent-fly. He was suddenly dripping with cold sweat, his mouth was full of the bitter taste of anger and his tongue felt stiff behind his teeth. Molly Welch, in a shirt-waist and a white tam-o'-shanter cap, slipped out from the tent under his arm and laughed up in his face. "She's a crazy one you brought along. She'll get what she wants!"

"Oh, I'll settle with you, all right!" Hedger brought out with difficulty.

"It's not my fault, Donnie. I couldn't do anything with her. She bought me off. What's the matter with you? Are you soft on her? She's safe enough. It's as easy as rolling off a log, if you keep cool." Molly Welch was rather excited herself, and she was chewing gum at a high speed as she stood beside him, looking up at the floating silver cone. "Now watch," she exclaimed suddenly. "She's coming down on the bar. I advised her to cut that out, but you see she does it first-rate. And she got rid of the skirt, too. Those black tights show off her legs very well. She keeps her feet together like I told her, and makes a good line along the back. See the light on those silver slippers, —that was a good idea I had. Come along to meet her. Don't be a grouch; she's done it fine!"

Molly tweaked his elbow, and then left him standing like a stump, while she ran down the beach with the crowd.

Though Hedger was sulking, his eye could not help seeing the low blue welter of the sea, the arrested bathers, standing in the surf, their arms and legs stained red by the dropping sun, all shading their eyes and gazing upward at the slowly falling silver star.

Molly Welch and the manager caught Eden under the arms and lifted her aside, a red page dashed up with a bouquet, and the band struck up "Blue Bell." Eden laughed and bowed, took Molly's arm, and ran up the sand in her black tights and silver slippers, dodging the friendly old women, and the gallant sports who wanted to offer their homage on the spot.

When she emerged from the tent, dressed in her own clothes, that part of the beach was almost deserted. She stepped to her companion's side and said carelessly: "Hadn't we better try to catch this boat? I hope you're not sore at me. Really, it was lots of fun."

Hedger looked at his watch. "Yes, we have fifteen minutes to get to the boat," he said politely.

As they walked toward the pier, one of the pages ran up panting. "Lady, you're carrying off the bouquet," he said, aggrievedly.

Eden stopped and looked at the bunch of spotty cotton roses in her hand. "Of course. I want them for a souvenir. You gave them to me yourself."

"I give 'em to you for looks, but you can't take 'em away. They belong to the show."

"Oh, you always use the same bunch?"

"Sure we do. There ain't too much money in this business."

She laughed and tossed them back to him. "Why are you angry?" she asked Hedger. "I wouldn't have done it if I'd been with some fellows, but I thought you were the sort who wouldn't mind. Molly didn't for a minute think you would."

"What possessed you to do such a fool thing?" he asked roughly.

"I don't know. When I saw her coming down, I wanted to try it. It looked exciting. Didn't I hold myself as well as she did?"

Hedger shrugged his shoulders, but in his heart he forgave her.

The return boat was not crowded, though the boats that passed them, going out, were packed to the rails. The sun was setting. Boys and girls sat on the long benches with their arms about each other, singing. Eden felt a strong wish to propitiate her companion, to be alone with him. She had been curiously wrought up by her balloon trip; it was a lark, but not very satisfying unless one came back to something after the flight. She wanted to be admired and adored. Though Eden said nothing, and sat with her arms limp on the rail in front of her, looking languidly at the rising silhouette of the city and the bright path of the sun, Hedger felt a strange drawing near to her. If he but brushed her white skirt with his knee, there was an instant communication between them, such as there had never been before. They did not talk at all, but when they went over the gangplank she took his arm and kept her shoulder close to his. He felt as if they were enveloped in a highly charged atmosphere, an invisible network of subtle, almost painful sensibility. They had somehow taken hold of each other.

An hour later, they were dining in the back garden of a little French hotel on Ninth Street, long since passed away. It was cool and leafy there, and the mosquitoes were not very numerous. A party of South Americans at another table were drinking champagne, and Eden murmured that she thought she would like some, if it were not too expensive. "Perhaps it will make me think I am in the balloon again. That was a very nice feeling. You've forgiven me, haven't you?"

Hedger gave her a quick straight look from under his black eyebrows, and something went over her that was like a chill, except that it was warm and feathery. She drank most of the wine; her companion was indifferent to it. He was talking more to her tonight than he had ever done before. She asked him about a new picture she had seen in his room; a queer thing full of stiff, supplicating female figures. "It's Indian, isn't it?"

"Yes. I call it Rain Spirits, or maybe, Indian Rain. In the Southwest, where I've been a good deal, the Indian traditions make women have to do with the rain-fall. They were supposed to control it, somehow, and to be able to find springs, and make moisture come out of the earth. You see I'm trying to learn to paint what people think and feel; to get away from all that photographic stuff. When I look at you, I don't see what a camera would see, do I?"

"How can I tell?"

"Well, if I should paint you, I could make you understand what I see." For the second time that day Hedger crimsoned unexpectedly, and his eyes fell and steadily contemplated a dish of little radishes. "That particular picture I got from a story a Mexican priest told me; he said he found it in an old manuscript book in a monastery down there, written by some Spanish Missionary, who got his stories from the Aztecs. This one he called 'The Forty Lovers of the Queen,' and it was more or less about rain-making."

"Aren't you going to tell it to me?" Eden asked.

Hedger fumbled among the radishes. "I don't know if it's the proper kind of story to tell a girl."

She smiled; "Oh, forget about that! I've been balloon riding today. I like to hear you talk."

Her low voice was flattering. She had seemed like clay in his hands ever since they got on the boat to come home. He leaned back in his chair, forgot his food, and, looking at her intently, began to tell his story, the theme of which he somehow felt was dangerous tonight.

The tale began, he said, somewhere in Ancient Mexico, and concerned the daughter of a king. The birth of this Princess was preceded by unusual portents. Three times her mother dreamed that she was delivered of serpents, which betokened that the child she carried would have power with the rain gods. The serpent was the symbol of water. The Princess grew up dedicated to the gods, and wise men taught her the rain-making mysteries. She was with difficulty restrained from men and was guarded at all times, for it was the law of the Thunder that she be maiden until her marriage. In the years of her adolescence, rain was abundant with her people. The oldest man could not remember such fertility. When the Princess had counted eighteen summers, her father went to drive out a war party that harried his borders on the north and troubled his prosperity. The King destroyed the invaders and brought home many prisoners. Among the prisoners was a young chief, taller than any of his captors, of such strength and ferocity that the King's people came a day's journey to look at him. When the Princess beheld his great stature, and saw that his arms and breast were covered with the figures of wild animals, bitten into the skin and coloured, she begged his life from her father. She desired that he should practise his art upon her, and prick upon her skin the signs of Rain and Lightning and Thunder, and stain the wounds with herb-juices, as they were upon his own body. For many days, upon the roof of the King's house, the Princess submitted herself to the bone needle, and the women with her marvelled at her fortitude. But the Princess was without shame before the Captive, and it came about that he threw from him his needles and his stains, and fell upon the Princess to violate her honour; and her women ran down from the roof screaming, to call the guard which stood at the gateway of the King's house, and none stayed to protect their mistress. When the guard came, the Captive was thrown into bonds, and he was gelded, and his tongue was torn out, and he was given for a slave to the Rain Princess.

The country of the Aztecs to the east was tormented by thirst, and their king, hearing much of the rain-making arts of the Princess, sent an embassy to her father, with presents and an offer of marriage. So the Princess went from her father to be the Queen of the Aztecs, and she took with her the Captive, who served her in everything with entire fidelity and slept upon a mat before her door.

The King gave his bride a fortress on the outskirts of the city, whither she retired to entreat the rain gods. This fortress was called the Queen's House, and on the night of the new moon the Queen came to it from the palace. But when the moon waxed and grew toward the round, because the god of Thunder had had his will of her, then the Queen returned to the King. Drought abated in the country and rain fell abundantly by reason of the Queen's power with the stars.

When the Queen went to her own house she took with her no servant but the Captive, and he slept outside her door and brought her food after she had fasted. The Queen had a jewel of great value, a turquoise that had fallen from the sun, and had the image of the sun upon it. And when she desired a young man whom she had seen in the army or among the slaves, she sent the

44

Captive to him with the jewel, for a sign that he should come to her secretly at the Queen's House upon business concerning the welfare of all. And some, after she had talked with them, she sent away with rewards; and some she took into her chamber and kept them by her for one night or two. Afterward she called the Captive and bade him conduct the youth by the secret way he had come, underneath the chambers of the fortress. But for the going away of the Queen's lovers the Captive took out the bar that was beneath a stone in the floor of the passage, and put in its stead a rush-reed, and the youth stepped upon it and fell through into a cavern that was the bed of an underground river, and whatever was thrown into it was not seen again. In this service nor in any other did the Captive fail the Queen.

But when the Queen sent for the Captain of the Archers, she detained him four days in her chamber, calling often for food and wine, and was greatly content with him. On the fourth day she went to the Captive outside her door and said: "Tomorrow take this man up by the sure way, by which the King comes, and let him live."

In the Queen's door were arrows, purple and white. When she desired the King to come to her publicly, with his guard, she sent him a white arrow; but when she sent the purple, he came secretly, and covered himself with his mantle to be hidden from the stone gods at the gate. On the fifth night that the Queen was with her lover, the Captive took a purple arrow to the King, and the King came secretly and found them together. He killed the Captain with his own hand, but the Queen he brought to public trial. The Captive, when he was put to the question, told on his fingers forty men that he had let through the underground passage into the river. The Captive and the Queen were put to death by fire, both on the same day, and afterward there was scarcity of rain.

Eden Bower sat shivering a little as she listened. Hedger was not trying to please her, she thought, but to antagonize and frighten her by his brutal story. She had often told herself that his lean, big-boned lower jaw was like his bull-dog's, but tonight his face made Caesar's most savage and determined expression seem an affectation. Now she was looking at the man he really was. Nobody's eyes had ever defied her like this. They were searching her and seeing everything; all she had concealed from Livingston, and from the millionaire and his friends, and from the newspaper men. He was testing her, trying her out, and she was more ill at ease than she wished to show.

"That's quite a thrilling story," she said at last, rising and winding her scarf about her throat. "It must be getting late. Almost every one has gone."

They walked down the Avenue like people who have quarrelled, or who wish to get rid of each other. Hedger did not take her arm at the street crossings, and they did not linger in the Square. At her door he tried none of the old devices of the Livingston boys. He stood like a post, having forgotten to take off his hat, gave her a harsh, threatening glance, muttered "goodnight," and shut his own door noisily.

There was no question of sleep for Eden Bower. Her brain was working like a machine that would never stop. After she undressed, she tried to calm her nerves by smoking a cigarette, lying on the divan by the open window. But she grew wider and wider awake, combating the challenge that had flamed all evening in Hedger's eyes. The balloon had been one kind of excitement, the wine another; but the thing that had roused her, as a blow rouses a proud man, was the doubt, the contempt, the sneering hostility with which the painter had looked at her when he told his savage story. Crowds and balloons were all very well, she reflected, but woman's chief adventure is man. With a mind over active and a sense of life over strong, she wanted to walk across the roofs in the starlight, to sail over the sea and face at once a world of which she had never been afraid.

Hedger must be asleep; his dog had stopped sniffing under the double doors. Eden put on her wrapper and slippers and stole softly down the hall over the old carpet; one loose board creaked just as she reached the ladder. The trapdoor was open, as always on hot nights. When she stepped out on the roof she drew a long breath and walked across it, looking up at the sky. Her foot touched something soft; she heard a low growl, and on the instant

Caesar's sharp little teeth caught her ankle and waited. His breath was like steam on her leg. Nobody had ever intruded upon his roof before, and he panted for the movement or the word that would let him spring his jaw. Instead, Hedger's hand seized his throat.

"Wait a minute. I'll settle with him," he said grimly. He dragged the dog toward the manhole and disappeared. When he came back, he found Eden standing over by the dark chimney, looking away in an offended attitude.

"I caned him unmercifully," he panted. "Of course you didn't hear anything; he never whines when I beat him. He didn't nip you, did he?"

"I don't know whether he broke the skin or not," she answered aggrievedly, still looking off into the west.

"If I were one of your friends in white pants, I'd strike a match to find whether you were hurt, though I know you are not, and then I'd see your ankle, wouldn't I?"

"I suppose so."

He shook his head and stood with his hands in the pockets of his old painting jacket. "I'm not up to such boy-tricks. If you want the place to yourself, I'll clear out. There are plenty of places where I can spend the night, what's left of it. But if you stay here and I stay here—" He shrugged his shoulders.

Eden did not stir, and she made no reply. Her head drooped slightly, as if she were considering. But the moment he put his arms about her they began to talk, both at once, as people do in an opera. The instant avowal brought out a flood of trivial admissions. Hedger confessed his crime, was reproached and forgiven, and now Eden knew what it was in his look that she had found so disturbing of late.

Standing against the black chimney, with the sky behind and blue shadows before, they looked like one of Hedger's own paintings of that period; two figures, one white and one dark, and nothing whatever distinguishable about them but that they were male and female. The faces were lost, the contours blurred in shadow, but the figures were a man and a woman, and that was their whole concern and their mysterious beauty,—it was the rhythm in which they moved, at last, along the roof and down into the dark hole; he first, drawing her gently after him. She came down very slowly. The excitement and bravado and uncertainty of that long day and night seemed all at once to tell upon her. When his feet were on the carpet and he reached up to lift her down, she twined her arms about his neck as after a long separation, and turned her face to him, and her lips, with their perfume of youth and passion.

One Saturday afternoon Hedger was sitting in the window of Eden's music room. They had been watching the pigeons come wheeling over the roofs from their unknown feeding grounds.

"Why," said Eden suddenly, "don't we fix those big doors into your studio so they will open? Then, if I want you, I won't have to go through the hall. That illustrator is loafing about a good deal of late."

"I'll open them, if you wish. The bolt is on your side."

"Isn't there one on yours, too?"

"No. I believe a man lived there for years before I came in, and the nurse used to have these rooms herself. Naturally, the lock was on the lady's side."

Eden laughed and began to examine the bolt. "It's all stuck up with paint." Looking about, her eye lighted upon a bronze Buddha which was one of the nurse's treasures. Taking him by his head, she struck the bolt a blow with his squatting posteriors. The two doors creaked, sagged, and swung weakly inward a little way, as if they were too old for such escapades. Eden tossed the heavy idol into a stuffed chair. "That's better," she exclaimed exultantly. "So the bolts are always on the lady's side? What a lot society takes for granted!"

Hedger laughed, sprang up and caught her arms roughly. "Whoever takes you for granted— Did anybody, ever?"

"Everybody does. That's why I'm here. You are the only one who knows anything about me. Now I'll have to dress if we're going out for dinner."

He lingered, keeping his hold on her. "But I won't always be the only one, Eden Bower. I won't be the last."

"No, I suppose not," she said carelessly. "But what does that matter? You are the first."

As a long, despairing whine broke in the warm stillness, they drew apart. Caesar, lying on his bed in the dark corner, had lifted his head at this invasion of sunlight, and realized that the side of his room was broken open, and his whole world shattered by change. There stood his master and this woman, laughing at him! The woman was pulling the long black hair of this mightiest of men, who bowed his head and permitted it.

VI

In time they quarrelled, of course, and about an abstraction,—as young people often do, as mature people almost never do. Eden came in late one afternoon. She had been with some of her musical friends to lunch at Burton Ives' studio, and she began telling Hedger about its splendours. He listened a moment and then threw down his brushes. "I know exactly what it's like," he said impatiently. "A very good department-store conception of a studio. It's one of the show places."

"Well, it's gorgeous, and he said I could bring you to see him. The boys tell me he's awfully kind about giving people a lift, and you might get something out of it."

Hedger started up and pushed his canvas out of the way. "What could I possibly get from Burton Ives? He's almost the worst painter in the world; the stupidest, I mean."

Eden was annoyed. Burton Ives had been very nice to her and had begged her to sit for him. "You must admit that he's a very successful one," she said coldly.

"Of course he is! Anybody can be successful who will do that sort of thing. I wouldn't paint his pictures for all the money in New York."

"Well, I saw a lot of them, and I think they are beautiful."

Hedger bowed stiffly.

"What's the use of being a great painter if nobody knows about you?" Eden went on persuasively. "Why don't you paint the kind of pictures people can understand, and then, after you're successful, do whatever you like?"

"As I look at it," said Hedger brusquely, "I am successful."

Eden glanced about. "Well, I don't see any evidences of it," she said, biting her lip. "He has a Japanese servant and a wine cellar, and keeps a riding horse."

Hedger melted a little. "My dear, I have the most expensive luxury in the world, and I am much more extravagant than Burton Ives, for I work to please nobody but myself."

"You mean you could make money and don't? That you don't try to get a public?"

"Exactly. A public only wants what has been done over and over. I'm painting for painters,—who haven't been born."

52

"What would you do if I brought Mr. Ives down here to see your things?"

"Well, for God's sake, don't! Before he left I'd probably tell him what I thought of him."

Eden rose. "I give you up. You know very well there's only one kind of success that's real."

"Yes, but it's not the kind you mean. So you've been thinking me a scrub painter, who needs a helping hand from some fashionable studio man? What the devil have you had anything to do with me for, then?"

"There's no use talking to you," said Eden walking slowly toward the door. "I've been trying to pull wires for you all afternoon, and this is what it comes to." She had expected that the tidings of a prospective call from the great man would be received very differently, and had been thinking as she came home in the stage how, as with a magic wand, she might gild Hedger's future, float him out of his dark hole on a tide of prosperity, see his name in the papers and his pictures in the windows on Fifth Avenue.

Hedger mechanically snapped the midsummer leash on Caesar's collar and they ran downstairs and hurried through Sullivan Street off toward the river. He wanted to be among rough, honest people, to get down where the big drays bumped over stone paving blocks and the men wore corduroy trowsers and kept their shirts open at the neck. He stopped for a drink in one of the sagging bar-rooms on the water front. He had never in his life been so deeply wounded; he did not know he could be so hurt. He had told this girl all his secrets. On the roof, in these warm, heavy summer nights, with her hands locked in his, he had been able to explain all his misty ideas about an unborn art the world was waiting for; had been able to explain them better than he had ever done to himself. And she had looked away to the chattels of this uptown studio and coveted them for him! To her he was only an unsuccessful Burton Ives.

Then why, as he had put it to her, did she take up with him? Young, beautiful, talented as she was, why had she wasted herself on a scrub? Pity? Hardly; she wasn't sentimental. There was no explaining her. But in this passion that had seemed so fearless and so fated to be, his own position now looked to him ridiculous; a poor dauber without money or fame,—it was her caprice to load him with favours. Hedger ground his teeth so loud that his dog, trotting beside him, heard him and looked up.

While they were having supper at the oysterman's, he planned his escape. Whenever he saw her again, everything he had told her, that he should never have told any one, would come back to him; ideas he had never whispered even to the painter whom he worshipped and had gone all the way to France to see. To her they must seem his apology for not having horses and a valet, or merely the puerile boastfulness of a weak man. Yet if she slipped the bolt tonight and came through the doors

and said, "Oh, weak man, I belong to you!" what could
he do? That was the danger. He would catch the train out
to Long Beach tonight, and tomorrow he would go on
to the north end of Long Island, where an old friend of
his had a summer studio among the sand dunes. He would
stay until things came right in his mind. And she could
find a smart painter, or take her punishment.

When he went home, Eden's room was dark; she was
dining out somewhere. He threw his things into a hold-
all he had carried about the world with him, strapped
up some colours and canvases, and ran downstairs.

VII

Five days later Hedger was a restless passenger on a
dirty, crowded Sunday train, coming back to town. Of
course he saw now how unreasonable he had been in
expecting a Huntington girl to know anything about pictures; here was a whole continent full of people who
knew nothing about pictures and he didn't hold it against
them. What had such things to do with him and Eden
Bower? When he lay out on the dunes, watching the
moon come up out of the sea, it had seemed to him that
there was no wonder in the world like the wonder of
Eden Bower. He was going back to her because she was
older than art, because she was the most overwhelming
thing that had ever come into his life.

He had written her yesterday, begging her to be at

home this evening, telling her that he was contrite, and wretched enough.

Now that he was on his way to her, his stronger feeling unaccountably changed to a mood that was playful and tender. He wanted to share everything with her, even the most trivial things. He wanted to tell her about the people on the train, coming back tired from their holiday with bunches of wilted flowers and dirty daisies; to tell her that the fish-man, to whom she had often sent him for lobsters, was among the passengers, disguised in a silk shirt and a spotted tie, and how his wife looked exactly like a fish, even to her eyes, on which cataracts were forming. He could tell her, too, that he hadn't as much as unstrapped his canvases,—that ought to convince her.

In those days passengers from Long Island came into New York by ferry. Hedger had to be quick about getting his dog out of the express car in order to catch the first boat. The East River, and the bridges, and the city to the west, were burning in the conflagration of the sunset; there was that great home-coming reach of evening in the air.

The car changes from Thirty-fourth Street were too many and too perplexing; for the first time in his life Hedger took a hansom cab for Washington Square. Caesar sat bolt upright on the worn leather cushion beside him, and they jogged off, looking down on the rest of the world.

It was twilight when they drove down lower Fifth Avenue into the Square, and through the Arch behind them were the two long rows of pale violet lights that used to bloom so beautifully against the grey stone and asphalt. Here and yonder about the Square hung globes that shed a radiance not unlike the blue mists of evening, emerging softly when daylight died, as the stars emerged in the thin blue sky. Under them the sharp shadows of the trees fell on the cracked pavement and the sleeping grass. The first stars and the first lights were growing silver against the gradual darkening, when Hedger paid his driver and went into the house,—which, thank God, was still there! On the hall table lay his letter of yesterday, unopened.

He went upstairs with every sort of fear and every sort of hope clutching at his heart; it was as if tigers were tearing him. Why was there no gas burning in the top hall? He found matches and the gas bracket. He knocked, but got no answer; nobody was there. Before his own door were exactly five bottles of milk, standing in a row. The milk-boy had taken spiteful pleasure in thus reminding him that he forgot to stop his order.

Hedger went down to the basement; it, too, was dark. The janitress was taking her evening airing on the basement steps. She sat waving a palm-leaf fan majestically, her dirty calico dress open at the neck. She told him at once that there had been "changes." Miss Bower's room was to let again, and the piano would go tomorrow. Yes,

she left yesterday, she sailed for Europe with friends
from Chicago. They arrived on Friday, heralded by
many telegrams. Very rich people they were said to be,
though the man had refused to pay the nurse a month's
rent in lieu of notice,—which would have been only right,
as the young lady had agreed to take the rooms until
October. Mrs. Foley had observed, too, that he didn't
overpay her or Willy for their trouble, and a great deal
of trouble they had been put to, certainly. Yes, the young
lady was very pleasant, but the nurse said there were
rings on the mahogany table where she had put tumblers
and wine glasses. It was just as well she was gone. The
Chicago man was uppish in his ways, but not much to
look at. She supposed he had poor health, for there was
nothing to him inside his clothes.

Hedger went slowly up the stairs—never had they
seemed so long, or his legs so heavy. The upper floor
was emptiness and silence. He unlocked his room, lit the
gas, and opened the windows. When he went to put his
coat in the closet, he found, hanging among his clothes,
a pale, flesh-tinted dressing gown he had liked to see her
wear, with a perfume—oh, a perfume that was still Eden
Bower! He shut the door behind him and there, in the
dark, for a moment he lost his manliness. It was when
he held this garment to him that he found a letter in the
pocket.

The note was written with a lead pencil, in haste: She
was sorry that he was angry, but she still didn't know

just what she had done. She had thought Mr. Ives would be useful to him; she guessed he was too proud. She wanted awfully to see him again, but Fate came knocking at her door after he had left her. She believed in Fate. She would never forget him, and she knew he would become the greatest painter in the world. Now she must pack. She hoped he wouldn't mind her leaving the dressing gown; somehow, she could never wear it again.

After Hedger read this, standing under the gas, he went back into the closet and knelt down before the wall; the knot hole had been plugged up with a ball of wet paper,—the same blue note-paper on which her letter was written.

He was hard hit. Tonight he had to bear the loneliness of a whole lifetime. Knowing himself so well, he could hardly believe that such a thing had ever happened to him, that such a woman had lain happy and contented in his arms. And now it was over. He turned out the light and sat down on his painter's stool before the big window. Caesar, on the floor beside him, rested his head on his master's knee. We must leave Hedger thus, sitting in his tank with his dog, looking up at the stars.

COMING, APHRODITE! This legend, in electric lights over the Lexington Opera House, had long announced the return of Eden Bower to New York after years of spectacular success in Paris. She came at last, under the management of an American Opera Company, but bringing her own *chef d'orchestre*.

One bright December afternoon Eden Bower was going down Fifth Avenue in her car, on the way to her broker, in Williams Street. Her thoughts were entirely upon stocks,—Cerro de Pasco, and how much she should buy of it,—when she suddenly looked up and realized that she was skirting Washington Square. She had not seen the place since she rolled out of it in an old-fashioned four-wheeler to seek her fortune, eighteen years ago.

"*Arrêtez, Alphonse. Attendez moi,*" she called, and opened the door before he could reach it. The children who were streaking over the asphalt on roller skates saw a lady in a long fur coat, and short, high-heeled shoes, alight from a French car and pace slowly about the Square, holding her muff to her chin. This spot, at least, had changed very little, she reflected; the same trees, the same fountain, the white arch, and over yonder, Garibaldi, drawing the sword for freedom. There, just opposite her, was the old red brick house.

"Yes, that is the place," she was thinking. "I can smell the carpets now, and the dog,—what was his name? That grubby bathroom at the end of the hall, and that dreadful Hedger—still, there was something about him, you know—" She glanced up and blinked against the sun. From somewhere in the crowded quarter south of the Square a flock of pigeons rose, wheeling quickly upward into the brilliant blue sky. She threw back her head, pressed her muff closer to her chin, and watched them with a smile of amazement and delight. So they still rose, out of all that dirt and noise and squalor, fleet and silvery, just as they used to rise that summer when she was twenty and went up in a balloon on Coney Island!

Alphonse opened the door and tucked her robes about her. All the way down town her mind wandered from Cerro de Pasco, and she kept smiling and looking up at the sky.

When she had finished her business with the broker, she asked him to look in the telephone book for the address of M. Gaston Jules, the picture dealer, and slipped the paper on which he wrote it into her glove. It was five o'clock when she reached the French Galleries, as they were called. On entering she gave the attendant her card, asking him to take it to M. Jules. The dealer appeared very promptly and begged her to come into his private office, where he pushed a great chair toward his desk for her and signalled his secretary to leave the room.

"How good your lighting is in here," she observed, glancing about. "I met you at Simon's studio, didn't I? Oh, no! I never forget anybody who interests me." She threw her muff on his writing table and sank into the deep chair. "I have come to you for some information that's not in my line. Do you know anything about an American painter named Hedger?"

He took the seat opposite her. "Don Hedger? But, certainly! There are some very interesting things of his in an exhibition at V——'s. If you would care to—"

She held up her hand. "No, no. I've no time to go to exhibitions. Is he a man of any importance?"

"Certainly. He is one of the first men among the moderns. That is to say, among the very moderns. He is always coming up with something different. He often exhibits in Paris, you must have seen—"

"No, I tell you I don't go to exhibitions. Has he had great success? That is what I want to know."

M. Jules pulled at his short grey moustache. "But, Madame, there are many kinds of success," he began cautiously.

Madame gave a dry laugh. "Yes, so he used to say. We once quarrelled on that issue. And how would you define his particular kind?"

M. Jules grew thoughtful. "He is a great name with all the young men, and he is decidedly an influence in art. But one can't definitely place a man who is original, erratic, and who is changing all the time."

She cut him short. "Is he much talked about at home? In Paris, I mean? Thanks. That's all I want to know." She rose and began buttoning her coat. "One doesn't like to have been an utter fool, even at twenty."

"*Mais, non!*" M. Jules handed her her muff with a quick, sympathetic glance. He followed her out through the carpeted show-room, now closed to the public and draped in cheesecloth, and put her into her car with words appreciative of the honour she had done him in calling.

Leaning back in the cushions, Eden Bower closed her eyes, and her face, as the street lamps flashed their ugly orange light upon it, became hard and settled, like a plaster cast; so a sail, that has been filled by a strong breeze, behaves when the wind suddenly dies. Tomorrow night the wind would blow again, and this mask would be the golden face of Aphrodite. But a "big" career takes its toll, even with the best of luck.

THE DIAMOND MINE

THE DIAMOND MINE

I

I first became aware that Cressida Garnet was on board when I saw young men with cameras going up to the boat deck. In that exposed spot she was good-naturedly posing for them—amid fluttering lavendar scarfs—wearing a most unseaworthy hat, her broad, vigorous face wreathed in smiles. She was too much an American not to believe in publicity. All advertising was good. If it was good for breakfast foods, it was good for prime donne,—especially for a prima donna who would never be any younger and who had just announced her intention of marrying a fourth time.

Only a few days before, when I was lunching with some friends at Sherry's, I had seen Jerome Brown come in with several younger men, looking so pleased and prosperous that I exclaimed upon it.

"His affairs," some one explained, "are looking up. He's going to marry Cressida Garnet. Nobody believed it at first, but since she confirms it he's getting all sorts of credit. That woman's a diamond mine."

If there was ever a man who needed a diamond mine at hand, immediately convenient, it was Jerome Brown. But as an old friend of Cressida Garnet, I was sorry to hear that mining operations were to be begun again.

I had been away from New York and had not seen Cressida for a year; now I paused on the gangplank to note how very like herself she still was, and with what undiminished zeal she went about even the most trifling things that pertained to her profession. From that distance I could recognize her "carrying" smile, and even what, in Columbus, we used to call "the Garnet look."

At the foot of the stairway leading up to the boat deck stood two of the factors in Cressida's destiny. One of them was her sister, Miss Julia; a woman of fifty with a relaxed, mournful face, an ageing skin that browned slowly, like meerschaum, and the unmistakable "look" by which one knew a Garnet. Beside her, pointedly ignoring her, smoking a cigarette while he ran over the passenger list with supercilious almond eyes, stood a youth in a pink shirt and a green plush hat, holding a French bull-dog on the leash. This was "Horace," Cressida's only son. He, at any rate, had not the Garnet look. He was rich and ruddy, indolent and insolent, with soft oval cheeks and the blooming complexion of twenty-two.

There was the beginning of a silky shadow on his upper lip. He seemed like a ripe fruit grown out of a rich soil; "oriental," his mother called his peculiar lusciousness. His aunt's restless and aggrieved glance kept flecking him from the side, but the two were as motionless as the *bouledogue*, standing there on his bench legs and surveying his travelling basket with loathing. They were waiting, in constrained immobility, for Cressida to descend and reanimate them,—will them to do or to be something. Forward, by the rail, I saw the stooped, eager back for which I was unconsciously looking: Miletus Poppas, the Greek Jew, Cressida's accompanist and shadow. We were all there, I thought with a smile, except Jerome Brown.

The first member of Cressida's party with whom I had speech was Mr. Poppas. When we were two hours out I came upon him in the act of dropping overboard a steamer cushion made of American flags. Cressida never sailed, I think, that one of these vivid comforts of travel did not reach her at the dock. Poppas recognized me just as the striped object left his hand. He was standing with his arm still extended over the rail, his fingers contemptuously sprung back. "Lest we forgedt!" he said with a shrug. "Does Madame Cressida know we are to have the pleasure of your company for this voyage?" He spoke deliberate, grammatical English—he despised the American rendering of the language—but there was an indescribably foreign quality in his voice,—a something muted; and though he aspirated his "th's" with such conscientious thoroughness, there was always the thud of a "d" in them. Poppas stood before me in a short, tightly buttoned grey coat and cap, exactly the colour of his greyish skin and hair and waxed moustache; a monocle on a very wide black ribbon dangled over his chest. As to his age, I could not offer a conjecture. In the twelve years I had known his thin lupine face behind Cressida's shoulder, it had not changed. I was used to his cold, supercilious manner, to his alarming, deep-set eyes,—very close together, in colour a yellowish green, and always gleaming with something like defeated fury, as if he were actually on the point of having it out with you, or with the world, at last.

I asked him if Cressida had engagements in London.

"Quite so; the Manchester Festival, some concerts at Queen's Hall, and the Opera at Covent Garden; a rather special production of the operas of Mozart. That she can still do quite well,—which is not at all, of course, what we might have expected, and only goes to show that our Madame Cressida is now, as always, a charming exception to rules." Poppas' tone about his client was consistently patronizing, and he was always trying to draw one into a conspiracy of two, based on a mutual understanding of her shortcomings.

I approached him on the one subject I could think of which was more personal than his usefulness to Cressida, and asked him whether he still suffered from facial neuralgia as much as he had done in former years, and whether he was therefore dreading London, where the climate used to be so bad for him.

"And is still," he caught me up, "And is still! For me to go to London is martyrdom, *chère Madame*. In New York it is bad enough, but in London it is the *auto da fé*, nothing less. My nervous system is exotic in any country washed by the Atlantic ocean, and it shivers like a little hairless dog from Mexico. It never relaxes. I think I have told you about my favourite city in the middle of Asia, *la sainte Asie*, where the rainfall is absolutely nil, and you are protected on every side by hundreds of metres of warm, dry sand. I was there when I was a child once, and it is still my intention to retire there when I have finished with all this. I would be there now, n-ow-ow," his voice rose querulously, "if Madame Cressida did not imagine that she needs me,—and her fancies, you know," he flourished his hands, "one gives in to them. In humouring her caprices you and I have already played some together."

We were approaching Cressida's deck chairs, ranged under the open windows of her stateroom. She was already recumbent, swathed in lavender scarfs and wearing purple orchids—doubtless from Jerome Brown. At her left, Horace had settled down to a French novel, and Julia Garnet, at her right, was complainingly regarding the grey horizon. On seeing me, Cressida struggled under her fur-lined robes and got to her feet,—which was more than Horace or Miss Julia managed to do. Miss Julia, as

I could have foretold, was not pleased. All the Garnets had an awkward manner with me. Whether it was that I reminded them of things they wished to forget, or whether they thought I esteemed Cressida too highly and the rest of them too lightly, I do not know; but my appearance upon their scene always put them greatly on their dignity. After Horace had offered me his chair and Miss Julia had said doubtfully that she thought I was looking rather better than when she last saw me, Cressida took my arm and walked me off toward the stern.

"Do you know, Carrie, I half wondered whether I shouldn't find you here, or in London, because you always turn up at critical moments in my life." She pressed my arm confidentially, and I felt that she was once more wrought up to a new purpose. I told her that I had heard some rumour of her engagement.

"It's quite true, and it's all that it should be," she reassured me. "I'll tell you about it later, and you'll see that it's a real solution. They are against me, of course,—all except Horace. He has been such a comfort."

Horace's support, such as it was, could always be had in exchange for his mother's signature, I suspected. The pale May day had turned bleak and chilly, and we sat down by an open hatchway which emitted warm air from somewhere below. At this close range I studied Cressida's face, and felt reassured of her unabated vitality; the old force of will was still there, and with it her characteristic optimism, the old hope of a "solution."

"You have been in Columbus lately?" she was saying. "No, you needn't tell me about it," with a sigh. "Why is it, Caroline, that there is so little of my life I would be willing to live over again? So little that I can even think of without depression. Yet I've really not such a bad conscience. It may mean that I still belong to the future more than to the past, do you think?"

My assent was not warm enough to fix her attention, and she went on thoughtfully: "Of course, it was a bleak country and a bleak period. But I've sometimes wondered whether the bleakness may not have been in me, too; for it has certainly followed me. There, that is no way to talk!" she drew herself up from a momentary attitude of dejection. "Sea air always lets me down at first. That's why it's so good for me in the end."

"I think Julia always lets you down, too," I said bluntly. "But perhaps that depression works out in the same way."

Cressida laughed. "Julia is rather more depressing than Georgie, isn't she? But it was Julia's turn. I can't come alone, and they've grown to expect it. They haven't, either of them, much else to expect."

At this point the deck steward approached us with a blue envelope. "A wireless for you, Madame Garnet."

Cressida put out her hand with impatience, thanked him graciously, and with every indication of pleasure tore open the blue envelope. "It's from Jerome Brown," she said with some confusion, as she folded the paper

small and tucked it between the buttons of her close-
fitting gown, "Something he forgot to tell me. How long
shall you be in London? Good; I want you to meet him.
We shall probably be married there as soon as my engagements are over." She rose. "Now I must write some
letters. Keep two places at your table, so that I can slip
away from my party and dine with you sometimes."

I walked with her toward her chair, in which Mr. Poppas was now reclining. He indicated his readiness to rise,
but she shook her head and entered the door of her deck
suite. As she passed him, his eye went over her with
assurance until it rested upon the folded bit of blue paper
in her corsage. He must have seen the original rectangle
in the steward's hand; having found it again, he dropped
back between Horace and Miss Julia, whom I think he
disliked no more than he did the rest of the world. He
liked Julia quite as well as he liked me, and he liked me
quite as well as he liked any of the women to whom he
would be fitfully agreeable upon the voyage. Once or
twice, during each crossing, he did his best and made
himself very charming indeed, to keep his hand in,—for
the same reason that he kept a dummy keyboard in his
stateroom, somewhere down in the bowels of the boat.
He practised all the small economies; paid the minimum
rate, and never took a deck chair, because, as Horace
was usually in the cardroom, he could sit in Horace's.

The three of them lay staring at the swell which was
steadily growing heavier. Both men had covered them-

selves with rugs, after dutifully bundling up Miss Julia. As I walked back and forth on the deck, I was struck by their various degrees of in-expressiveness. Opaque brown eyes, almond-shaped and only half open; wolfish green eyes, close-set and always doing something, with a crooked gleam boring in this direction or in that; watery grey eyes, like the thick edges of broken skylight glass: I would have given a great deal to know what was going on behind each pair of them.

These three were sitting there in a row because they were all woven into the pattern of one large and rather spendid life. Each had a bond, and each had a grievance. If they could have their will, what would they do with the generous, credulous creature who nourished them, I wondered? How deep a humiliation would each egotism exact? They would scarcely have harmed her in fortune or in person (though I think Miss Julia looked forward to the day when Cressida would "break" and could be mourned over),—but the fire at which she warmed herself, the little secret hope,—the illusion, ridiculous or sublime, which kept her going,—that they would have stamped out on the instant, with the whole Garnet pack behind them to make extinction sure. All, except, perhaps, Miletus Poppas. He was a vulture of the vulture race, and he had the beak of one. But I always felt that if ever he had her thus at his mercy,—if ever he came upon the softness that was hidden under so much hardness, the warm credulity under a life so dated and scheduled and "reported" and generally exposed,—he would hold his hand and spare.

The weather grew steadily rougher. Miss Julia at last plucked Poppas by the sleeve and indicated that she wished to be released from her wrappings. When she disappeared, there seemed to be every reason to hope that she might be off the scene for awhile. As Cressida said, if she had not brought Julia, she would have had to bring Georgie, or some other Garnet. Cressida's family was like that of the unpopular Prince of Wales, of whom, when he died, some wag wrote:

> *If it had been his brother,*
> *Better him than another.*
> *If it had been his sister,*
> *No one would have missed her.*

Miss Julia was dampening enough, but Miss Georgie was aggressive and intrusive. She was out to prove to the world, and more especially to Ohio, that all the Garnets were as like Cressida as two peas. Both sisters were club-women, social service workers, and directors in musical societies, and they were continually travelling up and down the Middle West to preside at meetings or to deliver addresses. They reminded one of two sombre, bumping electrics, rolling about with no visible means of locomotion, always running out of power and lying beached in some inconvenient spot until they received a check or a suggestion from Cressy. I was only too well acquainted with the strained, anxious expression that the sight of their handwriting brought to Cressida's face when she ran over her morning mail at breakfast. She usually put their letters by to read "when she was feeling up to it" and hastened to open others which might possibly contain something gracious or pleasant. Sometimes these family unburdenings lay about unread for several days. Any other letters would have got themselves lost, but these bulky epistles, never properly fitted to their envelopes, seemed immune to mischance and unfailingly disgorged to Cressida long explanations as to why her sisters had to do and to have certain things precisely upon her account and because she was so much a public personage.

The truth was that all the Garnets, and particularly her two sisters, were consumed by an habitual, bilious, unenterprising envy of Cressy. They never forgot that, no matter what she did for them or how far she dragged them about the world with her, she would never take one of them to live with her in her Tenth Street house in New York. They thought that was the thing they most wanted. But what they wanted, in the last analysis, was to *be* Cressida. For twenty years she had been plunged in struggle; fighting for her life at first, then for a beginning, for growth, and at last for eminence and perfection; fighting in the dark, and afterward in the light,—which, with her bad preparation, and with her uninspired youth already behind her, took even more courage. During those twenty years the Garnets had been comfortable and indo-

lent and vastly self-satisfied; and now they expected
Cressida to make them equal sharers in the finer rewards
of her struggle. When her brother Buchanan told me he
thought Cressida ought "to make herself one of them,"
he stated the converse of what he meant. They coveted
the qualities which had made her success, as well as the
benefits which came from it. More than her furs or her
fame or her fortune, they wanted her personal effective-
ness, her brighter glow and stronger will to live.

"Sometimes," I have heard Cressida say, looking up
from a bunch of those sloppily written letters, "sometimes I get discouraged."

For several days the rough weather kept Miss Julia
cloistered in Cressida's deck suite with the maid, Luisa,
who confided to me that the Signorina Garnet was "*difi-
cile*." After dinner I usually found Cressida unincum-
bered, as Horace was always in the cardroom and Mr.
Poppas either nursed his neuralgia or went through the
exercise of making himself interesting to some one of the
young women on board. One evening, the third night
out, when the sea was comparatively quiet and the sky
was full of broken black clouds, silvered by the moon
at their ragged edges, Cressida talked to me about Jerome
Brown.

I had known each of her former husbands. The first
one, Charley Wilton, Horace's father, was my cousin.
He was organist in a church in Columbus, and Cressida
married him when she was nineteen. He died of tubercu-

losis two years after Horace was born. Cressida nursed him through a long illness and made the living besides. Her courage during the three years of her first marriage was fine enough to foreshadow her future to any discerning eye, and it had made me feel that she deserved any number of chances at marital happiness. There had, of course, been a particular reason for each subsequent experiment, and a sufficiently alluring promise of success. Her motives, in the case of Jerome Brown, seemed to me more vague and less convincing than those which she had explained to me on former occasions.

"It's nothing hasty," she assured me. "It's been coming on for several years. He has never pushed me, but he was always there—some one to count on. Even when I used to meet him at the Whitings, while I was still singing at the Metropolitan, I always felt that he was different from the others; that if I were in straits of any kind, I could call on him. You can't know what that feeling means to me, Carrie. If you look back, you'll see it's something I've never had."

I admitted that, in so far as I knew, she had never been much addicted to leaning on people.

"I've never had any one to lean on," she said with a short laugh. Then she went on, quite seriously: "Somehow, my relations with people always become business relations in the end. I suppose it's because,—except for a sort of professional personality, which I've had to get, just as I've had to get so many other things,—I've not

79

very much that's personal to give people. I've had to give too much else. I've had to try too hard for people who wouldn't try at all."

"Which," I put in firmly, "has done them no good, and has robbed the people who really cared about you."

"By making me grubby, you mean?"

"By making you anxious and distracted so much of the time; empty."

She nodded mournfully. "Yes, I know. You used to warn me. Well, there's not one of my brothers and sisters who does not feel that I carried off the family success, just as I might have carried off the family silver,—if there'd been any! They take the view that there were just so many prizes in the bag; I reached in and took them, so there were none left for the others. At my age, that's a dismal truth to waken up to." Cressida reached for my hand and held it a moment, as if she needed courage to face the facts in her case. "When one remembers one's first success; how one hoped to go home like a Christmas tree full of presents— How much one learns in a lifetime! That year when Horace was a baby and Charley was dying, and I was touring the West with the Williams band, it was my feeling about my own people that made me go at all. Why I didn't drop myself into one of those muddy rivers, or turn on the gas in one of those dirty hotel rooms, I don't know to this day. At twenty-two you must hope for something more than to be able to bury your husband decently, and what I hoped for was to make my family happy. It was the same afterward in Germany. A young woman must live for human people. Horace wasn't enough. I might have had lovers, of course. I suppose you will say it would have been better if I had."

Though there seemed no need for me to say anything, I murmured that I thought there were more likely to be limits to the rapacity of a lover than to that of a discontented and envious family.

"Well," Cressida gathered herself up, "once I got out from under it all, didn't I? And perhaps, in a milder way, such a release can come again. You were the first person I told when I ran away with Charley, and for a long while you were the only one who knew about Blasius Bouchalka. That time, at least, I shook the Garnets. I wasn't distracted or empty. That time I was all there!"

"Yes," I echoed her, "that time you were all there. It's the greatest possible satisfaction to remember it."

"But even that," she sighed, "was nothing but lawyers and accounts in the end—and a hurt. A hurt that has lasted. I wonder what is the matter with me?"

The matter with Cressida was, that more than any woman I have ever known, she appealed to the acquisitive instinct in men; but this was not easily said, even in the brutal frankness of a long friendship.

We would probably have gone further into the Bouchalka chapter of her life, had not Horace appeared and nervously asked us if we did not wish to take a turn before we went inside. I pleaded indolence, but Cressida rose and disappeared with him. Later I came upon them, standing at the stern above the huddled steerage deck, which was by this time bathed in moonlight, under an almost clear sky. Down there on the silvery floor, little hillocks were scattered about under quilts and shawls; family units, presumably,—male, female, and young. Here and there a black shawl sat alone, nodding. They crouched submissively under the moonlight as if it were a spell. In one of those hillocks a baby was crying, but the sound was faint and thin, a slender protest which aroused no response. Everything was so still that I could hear snatches of the low talk between my friends. Cressida's voice was deep and entreating. She was remonstrating with Horace about his losses at bridge, begging him to keep away from the cardroom.

"But what else is there to do on a trip like this, my Lady?" he expostulated, tossing his spark of a cigarette-end overboard. "What is there, now, to do?"

"Oh, Horace!" she murmured, "how can you be so? If I were twenty-two, and a boy, with some one to back me—"

Horace drew his shoulders together and buttoned his top-coat. "Oh, I've not your energy, Mother dear. We make no secret of that. I am as I am. I didn't ask to be born into this charming world."

To this gallant speech Cressida made no answer. She

stood with her hand on the rail and her head bent forward, as if she had lost herself in thought. The ends of her scarf, lifted by the breeze, fluttered upward, almost transparent in the argent light. Presently she turned away,—as if she had been alone and were leaving only the night sea behind her,—and walked slowly forward; a strong, solitary figure on the white deck, the smoke-like scarf twisting and climbing and falling back upon itself in the light over her head. She reached the door of her stateroom and disappeared. Yes, she was a Garnet, but she was also Cressida; and she had done what she had done.

II

My first recollections of Cressida Garnet have to do with the Columbus Public Schools; a little girl with sunny brown hair and eager bright eyes, looking anxiously at the teacher and reciting the names and dates of the Presidents: "James Buchanan, 1857–1861; Abraham Lincoln, 1861–1865"; etc. Her family came from North Carolina, and they had that to feel superior about before they had Cressy. The Garnet "look," indeed, though based upon a strong family resemblance, was nothing more than the restless, preoccupied expression of an inflamed sense of importance. The father was a Democrat, in the sense that other men were doctors or lawyers. He scratched up some sort of poor living for his family behind office windows inscribed with the words "Real

Estate. Insurance. Investments." But it was his political faith that, in a Republican community, gave him his feeling of eminence and originality. The Garnet children were all in school then, scattered along from the first grade to the ninth. In almost any room of our school building you might chance to enter, you saw the self-conscious little face of one or another of them. They were restrained, uncomfortable children, not frankly boastful, but insinuating, and somehow forever demanding special consideration and holding grudges against teachers and classmates who did not show it them; all but Cressida, who was naturally as sunny and open as a May morning.

It was no wonder that Cressy ran away with young Charley Wilton, who hadn't a shabby thing about him except his health. He was her first music teacher, the choirmaster of the church in which she sang. Charley was very handsome; the "romantic" son of an old, impoverished family. He had refused to go into a good business with his uncles and had gone abroad to study music when that was an extravagant and picturesque thing for an Ohio boy to do. His letters home were handed round among the members of his own family and of other families equally conservative. Indeed, Charley and what his mother called "his music" were the romantic expression of a considerable group of people; young cousins and old aunts and quiet-dwelling neighbours, allied by the amity of several generations. Nobody was properly married in our part of Columbus unless Charley Wilton, and no other, played the wedding march. The old ladies of the First Church used to say that he "hovered over the keys like a spirit." At nineteen Cressida was beautiful enough to turn a much harder head than the pale, ethereal one Charley Wilton bent above the organ.

That the chapter which began so gracefully ran on into such a stretch of grim, hard prose, was simply Cressida's relentless bad luck. In her undertakings, in whatever she could lay hold of with her two hands, she was successful; but whatever happened to her was almost sure to be bad. Her family, her husbands, her son, would have crushed any other woman I have ever known. Cressida lived, more than most of us, "for others"; and what she seemed to promote among her beneficiaries was indolence and envy and discord—even dishonesty and turpitude.

Her sisters were fond of saying—at club luncheons— that Cressida had remained "untouched by the breath of scandal," which was not strictly true. There were captious people who objected to her long and close association with Miletus Poppas. Her second husband, Ransome McChord, the foreign representative of the great McChord Harvester Company, whom she married in Germany, had so persistently objected to Poppas that she was eventually forced to choose between them. Any one who knew her well could easily understand why she chose Poppas.

While her actual self was the least changed, the least modified by experience that it would be possible to imagine, there had been, professionally, two Cressida

Garnets; the big handsome girl, already a "popular favourite" of the concert stage, who took with her to Germany the raw material of a great voice;—and the accomplished artist who came back. The singer that returned was largely the work of Miletus Poppas. Cressida had at least known what she needed, hunted for it, found it, and held fast to it. After experimenting with a score of teachers and accompanists, she settled down to work her problem out with Poppas. Other coaches came and went —she was always trying new ones—but Poppas survived them all. Cressida was not musically intelligent; she never became so. Who does not remember the countless rehearsals which were necessary before she first sang *Isolde* in Berlin; the disgust of the conductor, the sullenness of the tenor, the rages of the blonde *teufelin*, boiling with the impatience of youth and genius, who sang her *Brangaena?* Everything but her driving power Cressida had to get from the outside.

Poppas was, in his way, quite as incomplete as his pupil. He possessed a great many valuable things for which there is no market; intuitions, discrimination, imagination, a whole twilight world of intentions and shadowy beginnings which were dark to Cressida. I remember that when "Trilby" was published she fell into a fright and said such books ought to be prohibited by law; which gave me an intimation of what their relationship had actually become.

Poppas was indispensable to her. He was like a book

in which she had written down more about herself than she could possibly remember—and it was information that she might need at any moment. He was the one person who knew her absolutely and who saw into the bottom of her grief. An artist's saddest secrets are those that have to do with his artistry. Poppas knew all the simple things that were so desperately hard for Cressida, all the difficult things in which she could count on herself; her stupidities and inconsistencies, the chiaroscuro of the voice itself and what could be expected from the mind somewhat mismated with it. He knew where she was sound and where she was mended. With him she could share the depressing knowledge of what a wretchedly faulty thing any productive faculty is.

But if Poppas was necessary to her career, she was his career. By the time Cressida left the Metropolitan Opera Company, Poppas was a rich man. He had always received a retaining fee and a percentage of her salary,—and he was a man of simple habits. Her liberality with Poppas was one of the weapons that Horace and the Garnets used against Cressida, and it was a point in the argument by which they justified to themselves their rapacity. Whatever they didn't get, they told themselves, Poppas would. What they got, therefore, they were only saving from Poppas. The Greek ached a good deal at the general pillage, and Cressida's conciliatory methods with her family made him sarcastic and spiteful. But he had to make terms, somehow, with the Garnets and

Horace, and with the husband, if there happened to be one. He sometimes reminded them, when they fell to wrangling, that they must not, after all, overturn the boat under them, and that it would be better to stop just before they drove her wild than just after. As he was the only one among them who understood the sources of her fortune,—and they knew it,—he was able, when it came to a general set-to, to proclaim sanctuary for the goose that laid the golden eggs.

That Poppas had caused the break between Cressida and McChord was another stick her sisters held over her. They pretended to understand perfectly, and were always explaining what they termed her "separation"; but they let Cressida know that it cast a shadow over her family and took a good deal of living down.

A beautiful soundness of body, a seemingly exhaustless vitality, and a certain "squareness" of character as well as of mind, gave Cressida Garnet earning powers that were exceptional even in her lavishly rewarded profession. Managers chose her over the heads of singers much more gifted, because she was so sane, so conscientious, and above all, because she was so sure. Her efficiency was like a beacon to lightly anchored men, and in the intervals between her marriages she had as many suitors as Penelope. Whatever else they saw in her at first, her competency so impressed and delighted them that they gradually lost sight of everything else. Her sterling character was the subject of her story. Once, as she said, she very nearly escaped her destiny. With Blasius Bouchalka she became almost another woman, but not quite. Her "principles," or his lack of them, drove those two apart in the end. It was of Bouchalka that we talked upon that last voyage I ever made with Cressida Garnet, and not of Jerome Brown. She remembered the Bohemian kindly, and since it was the passage in her life to which she most often reverted, it is the one I shall relate here.

III

Late one afternoon in the winter of 189–, Cressida and I were walking in Central Park after the first heavy storm of the year. The snow had been falling thickly all the night before, and all day, until about four o'clock. Then the air grew much warmer and the sky cleared. Overhead it was a soft, rainy blue, and to the west a smoky gold. All around the horizon everything became misty and silvery; even the big, brutal buildings looked like pale violet water-colours on a silver ground. Under the elm trees along the Mall the air was purple as wisterias. The sheep-field, toward Broadway, was smooth and white, with a thin gold wash over it. At five o'clock the carriage came for us, but Cressida sent the driver home to the Tenth Street house with the message that she would dine uptown, and that Horace and Mr. Poppas were not to wait for her. As the horses trotted away we turned up the Mall.

"I won't go indoors this evening for any one," Cressida declared. "Not while the sky is like that. Now we will go back to the laurel wood. They are so black, over the snow, that I could cry for joy. I don't know when I've felt so care-free as I feel tonight. Country winter, country stars—they always make me think of Charley Wilton."

She was singing twice a week, sometimes oftener, at the Metropolitan that season, quite at the flood-tide of her powers, and so enmeshed in operatic routine that to be walking in the park at an unaccustomed hour, unattended by one of the men of her entourage, seemed adventurous. As we strolled along the little paths among the snow banks and the bronze laurel bushes, she kept going back to my poor young cousin, dead so long. "Things happen out of season. That's the worst of living. It was untimely for both of us, and yet," she sighed softly, "since he had to die, I'm not sorry. There was one beautifully happy year, though we were so poor, and it gave him—something! It would have been too hard if he'd had to miss everything." (I remember her simplicity, which never changed any more than winter or Ohio change.) "Yes," she went on, "I always feel very tenderly about Charley. I believe I'd do the same thing right over again, even knowing all that had to come after. If I were nineteen tonight, I'd rather go sleigh-riding with Charley Wilton than anything else I've ever done."

We walked until the procession of carriages on the driveway, getting people home to dinner, grew thin, and then we went slowly toward the Seventh Avenue gate, still talking of Charley Wilton. We decided to dine at a place not far away, where the only access from the street was a narrow door, like a hole in the wall, between a tobacconist's and a flower shop. Cressida deluded herself into believing that her incognito was more successful in such non-descript places. She was wearing a long sable coat, and a deep fur hat, hung with red cherries, which she had brought from Russia. Her walk had given her a fine colour, and she looked so much a personage that no disguise could have been wholly effective.

The dining-rooms, frescoed with conventional Italian scenes, were built round a court. The orchestra was playing as we entered and selected our table. It was not a bad orchestra, and we were no sooner seated than the first violin began to speak, to assert itself, as if it were suddenly done with mediocrity.

"We have been recognized," Cressida said complacently. "What a good tone he has, quite unusual. What does he look like?" She sat with her back to the musicians.

The violinist was standing, directing his men with his head and with the beak of his violin. He was a tall, gaunt young man, big-boned and rugged, in skin-tight clothes. His high forehead had a kind of luminous pallour, and his hair was jet black and somewhat stringy. His manner was excited and dramatic. At the end of the number he acknowledged the applause, and Cressida looked at him graciously over her shoulder. He swept her with a brilliant glance and bowed again. Then I noticed his red lips and thick black eyebrows.

"He looks as if he were poor or in trouble," Cressida said. "See how short his sleeves are, and how he mops his face as if the least thing upset him. This is a hard winter for musicians."

The violinist rummaged among some music piled on a chair, turning over the sheets with flurried rapidity, as if he were searching for a lost article of which he was in desperate need. Presently he placed some sheets upon the piano and began vehemently to explain something to the pianist. The pianist stared at the music doubtfully—he was a plump old man with a rosy, bald crown, and his shiny linen and neat tie made him look as if he were on his way to a party. The violinist bent over him, suggesting rhythms with his shoulders and running his bony finger up and down the pages. When he stepped back to his place, I noticed that the other players sat at ease, without raising their instruments.

"He is going to try something unusual," I commented. "It looks as if it might be manuscript."

It was something, at all events, that neither of us had heard before, though it was very much in the manner of the later Russian composers who were just beginning to be heard in New York. The young man made a brilliant dash of it, despite a lagging, scrambling accompaniment by the conservative pianist. This time we both applauded him vigorously and again, as he bowed, he swept us with his eye.

The usual repertory of restaurant music followed, varied by a charming bit from Massenet's "Manon," then little known in this country. After we paid our check, Cressida took out one of her visiting cards and wrote across the top of it: "*We thank you for the unusual music and the pleasure your playing has given us.*" She folded the card in the middle, and asked the waiter to give it to the director of the orchestra. Pausing at the door, while the porter dashed out to call a cab, we saw, in the wall mirror, a pair of wild black eyes following us quite despairingly from behind the palms at the other end of the room. Cressida observed as we went out that the young man was probably having a hard struggle. "He never got those clothes here, surely. They were probably made by a country tailor in some little town in Austria. He seemed wild enough to grab at anything, and was trying to make himself heard above the dishes, poor fellow. There are so many like him. I wish I could help them all! I didn't quite have the courage to send him money. His smile, when he bowed to us, was not that of one who would take it, do you think?"

"No," I admitted, "it wasn't. He seemed to be pleading for recognition. I don't think it was money he wanted."

A week later I came upon some curious-looking manuscript songs on the piano in Cressida's music room. The text was in some Slavic tongue with a French translation written underneath. Both the handwriting and the musical script were done in a manner experienced, even distinguished. I was looking at them when Cressida came in.

"Oh, yes!" she exclaimed. "I meant to ask you to try them over. Poppas thinks they are very interesting. They are from that young violinist, you remember,—the one we noticed in the restaurant that evening. He sent them with such a nice letter. His name is Blasius Bouchalka (Boú-kal-ka), a Bohemian."

I sat down at the piano and busied myself with the manuscript, while Cressida dashed off necessary notes and wrote checks in a large square checkbook, six to a page. I supposed her immersed in sumptuary preoccupations when she suddenly looked over her shoulder and said, "Yes, that legend, *Sarka*, is the most interesting. Run it through a few times and I'll try it over with you."

There was another, "*Dans les ombres des fôrets tristes*," which I thought quite as beautiful. They were fine songs; very individual, and each had that spontaneity which makes a song seem inevitable and, once for all, "done." The accompaniments were difficult, but not unnecessarily so; they were free from fatuous ingenuity and fine writing.

"I wish he'd indicated his tempi a little more clearly," I remarked as I finished *Sarka* for the third time. "It matters, because he really has something to say. An orchestral accompaniment would be better, I should think."

"Yes, he sent the orchestral arrangement. Poppas has it. It works out beautifully,—so much colour in the instrumentation. The English horn comes in so effectively there," she rose and indicated the passage, "just right with the voice. I've asked him to come next Sunday, so please be here if you can. I want to know what you think of him."

Cressida was always at home to her friends on Sunday afternoon unless she was billed for the evening concert at the Opera House, in which case we were sufficiently advised by the daily press. Bouchalka must have been told to come early, for when I arrived on Sunday, at four, he and Cressida had the music-room quite to themselves and were standing by the piano in earnest conversation. In a few moments they were separated by other early comers, and I led Bouchalka across the hall to the drawing-room. The guests, as they came in, glanced at him curiously. He wore a dark blue suit, soft and rather baggy, with a short coat, and a high double-breasted vest with two rows of buttons coming up to the loops of his black tie. This costume was even more foreign-looking than his skin-tight dress clothes, but it was more becoming. He spoke hurried, elliptical English, and very good French. All his sympathies were French rather than German—the Czecks lean to the one culture or to the other. I found him a fierce, a transfixing talker. His brilliant eyes, his gaunt hands, his white, deeply-lined forehead, all entered into his speech.

I asked him whether he had not recognized Madame Garnet at once when we entered the restaurant that evening more than a week ago.

"*Mais, certainement!* I hear her twice when she sings in the afternoon, and sometimes at night for the last act. I have a friend who buys a ticket for the first part, and he comes out and gives to me his pass-back check, and I return for the last act. That is convenient if I am broke." He explained the trick with amusement but without embarrassment, as if it were a shift that we might any of us be put to.

I told him that I admired his skill with the violin, but his songs much more.

He threw out his red under-lip and frowned. "Oh, I have no instrument! The violin I play from necessity; the flute, the piano, as it happens. For three years now I write all the time, and it spoils the hand for violin."

When the maid brought him his tea, he took both muffins and cakes and told me that he was very hungry. He had to lunch and dine at the place where he played, and he got very tired of the food. "But since," his black eyebrows nearly met in an acute angle, "but since, before, I eat at a bakery, with the slender brown roach on the pie, I guess I better let alone well enough." He paused to drink his tea; as he tasted one of the cakes his face lit with sudden animation and he gazed across the hall after the maid with the tray—she was now holding it before the aged and ossified 'cellist of the Hempfstangle Quartette. "*Des gâteaux*," he murmured feelingly, "*ou est-ce qu'elle peut trouver de tels gâteaux ici à* New York?"

I explained to him that Madame Garnet had an accomplished cook who made them,—an Austrian, I thought.

He shook his head. "*Austrichienne? Je ne pense pas.*"

Cressida was approaching with the new Spanish soprano, Mme. Bartolas, who was all black velvet and long black feathers, with a lace veil over her rich pallour and even a little black patch on her chin. I beckoned them. "Tell me, Cressida, isn't Ruzenka an Austrian?"

She looked surprised. "No, a Bohemian, though I got her in Vienna." Bouchalka's expression, and the remnant of a cake in his long fingers, gave her the connection. She laughed. "You like them? Of course, they are of your own country. You shall have more of them." She nodded and went away to greet a guest who had just come in.

A few moments later, Horace, then a beautiful lad in Eton clothes, brought another cup of tea and a plate of cakes for Bouchalka. We sat down in a corner, and talked about his songs. He was neither boastful nor deprecatory. He knew exactly in what respects they were excellent. I decided as I watched his face, that he must be under thirty. The deep lines in his forehead probably came there from his habit of frowning densely when he struggled to express himself, and suddenly elevating his coal-black eyebrows when his ideas cleared. His teeth were white, very irregular and interesting. The corrective methods of modern dentistry would have taken away half his good looks. His mouth would have been much less attractive for any re-arranging of those long, narrow, over-crowded teeth. Along with his frown and his way of thrusting out his lip, they contributed, somehow, to the engaging impetuousness of his conversation. As we talked about his songs, his manner changed. Before that he had seemed responsive and easily pleased. Now he grew abstracted, as if I had taken away his pleasant afternoon and wakened him to his miseries. He moved restlessly in his clothes. When I mentioned Puccini, he held his head in his hands. "Why is it they like that always and always? A little, oh yes, very nice. But so much, always the same thing! Why?" He pierced me with the despairing glance which had followed us out of the restaurant.

I asked him whether he had sent any of his songs to the publishers and named one whom I knew to be discriminating. He shrugged his shoulders. "They not want Bohemian songs. They not want my music. Even the street cars will not stop for me here, like for other people. Every time, I wait on the corner until somebody else make a signal to the car, and then it stop,—but not for me."

Most people cannot become utterly poor; whatever happens, they can right themselves a little. But one felt that Bouchalka was the sort of person who might actually starve or blow his brains out. Something very important had been left out either of his make-up or of his education; something that we are not accustomed to miss in people.

Gradually the parlour was filled with little groups of friends, and I took Bouchalka back to the music-room where Cressida was surrounded by her guests; feathered women, with large sleeves and hats, young men of no importance, in frock coats, with shining hair, and the smile which is intended to say so many flattering things but which really expresses little more than a desire to get on. The older men were standing about waiting for a word *à deux* with the hostess. To these people Bouchalka had nothing to say. He stood stiffly at the outer edge of the circle, watching Cressida with intent, impatient eyes, until, under the pretext of showing him a score, she drew him into the alcove at the back end of the long room, where she kept her musical library. The bookcases ran from the floor to the ceiling. There was a table and a reading-lamp, and a window seat looking upon the little walled garden. Two persons could be quite withdrawn there, and yet be a part of the general friendly scene. Cressida took a score from the shelf, and sat down with Bouchalka upon the window seat, the book open between them, though neither of them looked at it again. They fell to talking with great earnestness. At last the Bohemian pulled out a large, yellowing silver watch, held it up before him, and stared at it a moment as if it were an object of horror. He sprang up, bent over Cressida's hand and murmured something, dashed into the hall and out of the front door without waiting for the maid to open it. He had worn no overcoat, apparently. It was then seven o'clock; he would surely be late at his post in the up-town restaurant. I hoped he would have wit enough to take the elevated.

After supper Cressida told me his story. His parents, both poor musicians,—the mother a singer—died while he was yet a baby, and he was left to the care of an arbitrary uncle who resolved to make a priest of him. He was put into a monastery school and kept there. The organist and choir-director, fortunately for Blasius, was an excellent musician, a man who had begun his career brilliantly, but who had met with crushing sorrows and disappointments in the world. He devoted himself to his talented pupil, and was the only teacher the young man ever had. At twenty-one, when he was ready for the novitiate, Blasius felt that the call of life was too strong for him, and he ran away out into a world of which he knew nothing. He tramped southward to Vienna, begging and playing his fiddle from town to town. In Vienna he fell in with a gipsy band which was being recruited for a Paris restaurant and went with them to Paris. He played in cafés and in cheap theatres, did transcribing for a music publisher, tried to get pupils. For four years he was the mouse, and hunger was the cat. She kept him on the jump. When he got work he did not understand why; when he lost a job he did not understand why. During the time when most of us acquire a practical sense, get a half-unconscious knowledge of hard facts and market values, he had been shut away from the world, fed like the pigeons in the bell-tower of his monastery. Bouchalka had now been in New York a year, and for all he knew about it, Cressida said, he might have landed the day before yesterday.

Several weeks went by, and as Bouchalka did not reappear on Tenth Street, Cressida and I went once more to the place where he had played, only to find another violinist leading the orchestra. We summoned the proprietor, a Swiss-Italian, polite and solicitous. He told us the gentleman was not playing there any more,—was playing somewhere else, but he had forgotten where. We insisted upon talking to the old pianist, who at last reluctantly admitted that the Bohemian had been dismissed. He had arrived very late one Sunday night three weeks ago, and had hot words with the proprietor. He had been late before, and had been warned. He was a very talented fellow, but wild and not to be depended upon. The old man gave us the address of a French boarding-house on Seventh Avenue where Bouchalka used to room. We drove there at once, but the woman who kept the place said that he had gone away two weeks before, leaving no address, as he never got letters. Another Bohemian, who did engraving on glass, had a room with her, and when he came home perhaps he could tell where Bouchalka was, for they were friends.

It took us several days to run Bouchalka down, but

when we did find him Cressida promptly busied herself
in his behalf. She sang his "*Sarka*" with the Metropolitan
Opera orchestra at a Sunday night concert, she got him a
position with the Symphony Orchestra, and persuaded
the conservative Hempfstangle Quartette to play one of
his chamber compositions from manuscript. She aroused
the interest of a publisher in his work, and introduced
him to people who were helpful to him.

By the new year Bouchalka was fairly on his feet. He
had proper clothes now, and Cressida's friends found
him attractive. He was usually at her house on Sunday
afternoons; so usually, indeed, that Poppas began pointedly to absent himself. When other guests arrived, the
Bohemian and his patroness were always found at the
critical point of discussion,—at the piano, by the fire, in
the alcove at the end of the room—both of them interested
and animated. He was invariably respectful and admiring,
deferring to her in every tone and gesture, and she was
perceptibly pleased and flattered,—as if all this were new
to her and she were tasting the sweetness of a first success.

One wild day in March Cressida burst tempestuously
into my apartment and threw herself down, declaring
that she had just come from the most trying rehearsal she
had ever lived through. When I tried to question her
about it, she replied absently and continued to shiver and
crouch by the fire. Suddenly she rose, walked to the window, and stood looking out over the Square, glittering

with ice and rain and strewn with the wrecks of umbrellas. When she turned again, she approached me with determination.

"I shall have to ask you to go with me," she said firmly. "That crazy Bouchalka has gone and got a pleurisy or something. It may be pneumonia; there is an epidemic of it just now. I've sent Dr. Brooks to him, but I can never tell anything from what a doctor says. I've got to see Bouchalka and his nurse, and what sort of place he's in. I've been rehearsing all day and I'm singing tomorrow night; I can't have so much on my mind. Can you come with me? It will save time in the end."

I put on my furs, and we went down to Cressida's carriage, waiting below. She gave the driver a number on Seventh Avenue, and then began feeling her throat with the alarmed expression which meant that she was not going to talk. We drove in silence to the address, and by this time it was growing dark. The French landlady was a cordial, comfortable person who took Cressida in at a glance and seemed much impressed. Cressida's incognito was never successful. Her black gown was inconspicuous enough, but over it she wore a dark purple velvet carriage coat, lined with fur and furred at the cuffs and collar. The Frenchwoman's eye ran over it delightedly and scrutinized the veil which only half-concealed the well-known face behind it. She insisted upon conducting us up to the fourth floor herself, running ahead of us and turning up the gas jets in the dark, musty-smelling halls. I suspect that she tarried outside the door after we sent the nurse for her walk.

We found the sick man in a great walnut bed, a relic of the better days which this lodging house must have seen. The grimy red plush carpet, the red velvet chairs with broken springs, the double gilt-framed mirror above the mantel, had all been respectable, substantial contributions to comfort in their time. The fireplace was now empty and grateless, and an ill-smelling gas stove burned in its sooty recess under the cracked marble. The huge arched windows were hung with heavy red curtains, pinned together and lightly stirred by the wind which rattled the loose frames.

I was examining these things while Cressida bent over Bouchalka. Her carriage cloak she threw over the foot of his bed, either from a protective impulse, or because there was no place else to put it. After she had greeted him and seated herself, the sick man reached down and drew the cloak up over him, looking at it with weak, childish pleasure and stroking the velvet with his long fingers. "*Couleur de gloire, couleur des reines!*" I heard him murmur. He thrust the sleeve under his chin and closed his eyes. His loud, rapid breathing was the only sound in the room. If Cressida brushed back his hair or touched his hand, he looked up long enough to give her a smile of utter adoration, naïve and uninquiring, as if he were smiling at a dream or a miracle.

The nurse was gone for an hour, and we sat quietly,

Cressida with her eyes fixed on Bouchalka, and I absorbed in the strange atmosphere of the house, which seemed to seep in under the door and through the walls. Occasionally we heard a call for "*de l'eau chaude!*" and the heavy trot of a serving woman on the stairs. On the floor below somebody was struggling with Schubert's Marche Militaire on a coarse-toned upright piano. Sometimes, when a door was opened, one could hear a parrot screaming, "*Voilà, voilà, tonnerre!*" The house was built before 1870, as one could tell from windows and mouldings, and the walls were thick. The sounds were not disturbing and Bouchalka was probably used to them.

When the nurse returned and we rose to go, Bouchalka still lay with his cheek on her cloak, and Cressida left it. "It seems to please him," she murmured as we went down the stairs. "I can go home without a wrap. It's not far." I had, of course, to give her my furs, as I was not singing *Donna Anna* tomorrow evening and she was.

After this I was not surprised by any devout attitude in which I happened to find the Bohemian when I entered Cressida's music-room unannounced, or by any radiance on her face when she rose from the window-seat in the alcove and came down the room to greet me.

Bouchalka was, of course, very often at the Opera now. On almost any night when Cressida sang, one could see his narrow black head—high above the temples and rather constrained behind the ears—peering from some part of the house. I used to wonder what he thought of

Cressida as an artist, but probably he did not think seriously at all. A great voice, a handsome woman, a great prestige, all added together made a "great artist," the common synonym for success. Her success, and the material evidences of it, quite blinded him. I could never draw from him anything adequate about Anna Straka, Cressida's Slavic rival, and this perhaps meant that he considered comparison disloyal. All the while that Cressida was singing reliably, and satisfying the management, Straka was singing uncertainly and making history. Her voice was primarily defective, and her immediate vocal method was bad. Cressida was always living up to her contract, delivering the whole order in good condition; while the Slav was sometimes almost voiceless, sometimes inspired. She put you off with a hope, a promise, time after time. But she was quite as likely to put you off with a revelation,—with an interpretation that was inimitable, unrepeatable.

Bouchalka was not a reflective person. He had his own idea of what a great prima donna should be like, and he took it for granted that Mme. Garnet corresponded to his conception. The curious thing was that he managed to impress his idea upon Cressida herself. She began to see herself as he saw her, to try to be like the notion of her that he carried somewhere in that pointed head of his. She was exalted quite beyond herself. Things that had been chilled under the grind came to life in her that winter, with the breath of Bouchalka's adoration. Then,

if ever in her life, she heard the bird sing on the branch
outside her window; and she wished she were younger,
lovelier, freer. She wished there were no Poppas, no
Horace, no Garnets. She longed to be only the bewitch-
ing creature Bouchalka imagined her.

One April day when we were driving in the Park,
Cressida, superb in a green-and-primrose costume hurried over from Paris, turned to me smiling and said: "Do
you know, this is the first spring I haven't dreaded. It's
the first one I've ever really had. Perhaps people never
have more than one, whether it comes early or late."
She told me that she was overwhelmingly in love.

Our visit to Bouchalka when he was ill had, of course,
been reported, and the men about the Opera House had
made of it the only story they have the wit to invent.
They could no more change the pattern of that story
than the spider could change the design of its web. But
being, as she said, "in love" suggested to Cressida only
one plan of action; to have the Tenth Street house done
over, to put more money into her brothers' business, send
Horace to school, raise Poppas' percentage, and then
with a clear conscience be married in the Church of the
Ascension. She went through this program with her usual
thoroughness. She was married in June and sailed immediately with her husband. Poppas was to join them in
Vienna in August, when she would begin to work again.
From her letters I gathered that all was going well, even
beyond her hopes.

When they returned in October, both Cressida and Blasius seemed changed for the better. She was perceptibly freshened and renewed. She attacked her work at once with more vigour and more ease; did not drive herself so relentlessly. A little carelessness became her wonderfully. Bouchalka was less gaunt, and much less flighty and perverse. His frank pleasure in the comfort and order of his wife's establishment was ingratiating, even if it was a little amusing. Cressida had the sewing-room at the top of the house made over into a study for him. When I went up there to see him, I usually found him sitting before the fire or walking about with his hands in his coat pockets, admiring his new possessions. He explained the ingenious arrangement of his study to me a dozen times.

With Cressida's friends and guests, Bouchalka assumed nothing for himself. His deportment amounted to a quiet, unobtrusive appreciation of her and of his good fortune. He was proud to owe his wife so much. Cressida's Sunday afternoons were more popular than ever, since she herself had so much more heart for them. Bouchalka's picturesque presence stimulated her graciousness and charm. One still found them conversing together as eagerly as in the days when they saw each other but seldom. Consequently their guests were never bored. We felt as if the Tenth Street house had a pleasant climate quite its own. In the spring, when the Metropolitan company went on tour, Cressida's husband accompanied her, and afterward they again sailed for Genoa.

During the second winter people began to say that Bouchalka was becoming too thoroughly domesticated, and that since he was growing heavier in body he was less attractive. I noticed his increasing reluctance to stir abroad. Nobody could say that he was "wild" now. He seemed to dread leaving the house, even for an evening. Why should he go out, he said, when he had everything he wanted at home? He published very little. One was given to understand that he was writing an opera. He lived in the Tenth Street house like a tropical plant under glass. Nowhere in New York could he get such cookery as Ruzenka's. Ruzenka ("little Rose") had, like her mistress, bloomed afresh, now that she had a man and a compatriot to cook for. Her invention was tireless, and she took things with a high hand in the kitchen, confident of a perfect appreciation. She was a plump, fair, blue-eyed girl, giggly and easily flattered, with teeth like cream. She was passionately domestic, and her mind was full of homely stories and proverbs and superstitions which she somehow worked into her cookery. She and Bouchalka had between them a whole literature of traditions about sauces and fish and pastry. The cellar was full of the wines he liked, and Ruzenka always knew what wines to serve with the dinner. Blasius' monastery had been famous for good living.

That winter was a very cold one, and I think the even temperature of the house enslaved Bouchalka. "Imagine it," he once said to me when I dropped in during a blinding snowstorm and found him reading before the fire. "To be warm all the time, every day! It is like Aladdin. In Paris I have had weeks together when I was not warm once, when I did not have a bath once, like the cats in the street. The nights were a misery. People have terrible dreams when they are so cold. Here I waken up in the night so warm I do not know what it means. Her door is open, and I turn on my light. I cannot believe in myself until I see that she is there."

I began to think that Bouchalka's wildness had been the desperation which the tamest animals exhibit when they are tortured or terrorized. Naturally luxurious, he had suffered more than most men under the pinch of penury. Those first beautiful compositions, full of the folk-music of his own country, had been wrung out of him by home-sickness and heart-ache. I wondered whether he could compose only under the spur of hunger and loneliness, and whether his talent might not subside with his despair. Some such apprehension must have troubled Cressida, though his gratitude would have been propitiatory to a more exacting task-master. She had always liked to make people happy, and he was the first one who had accepted her bounty without sourness. When he did not accompany her upon her spring tour, Cressida said it was because travelling interfered with composition; but I felt that she was deeply disappointed. Blasius, or Blažej, as his wife had with difficulty learned to call him, was not showy or extravagant. He hated hotels, even the best of them. Cressida had always fought for the hearthstone and the fireside, and the humour of Destiny is sometimes to give us too much of what we desire. I believe she would have preferred even enthusiasm about other women to his utter *oisiveté*. It was his old fire, not his docility, that had won her.

During the third season after her marriage Cressida had only twenty-five performances at the Metropolitan, and she was singing out of town a great deal. Her husband did not bestir himself to accompany her, but he attended, very faithfully, to her correspondence and to her business at home. He had no ambitious schemes to increase her fortune, and he carried out her directions exactly. Nevertheless, Cressida faced her concert tours somewhat grimly, and she seldom talked now about their plans for the future.

The crisis in this growing estrangement came about by accident,—one of those chance occurrences that affect our lives more than years of ordered effort,—and it came in an inverted form of a situation old to comedy. Cressida had been on the road for several weeks; singing in Minneapolis, Cleveland, St. Paul, then up into Canada and back to Boston. From Boston she was to go directly to Chicago, coming down on the five o'clock train and taking the eleven, over the Lake Shore, for the West. By her schedule she would have time to change cars comfortably at the Grand Central station.

On the journey down from Boston she was seized with a great desire to see Blasius. She decided, against her custom, one might say against her principles, to risk a performance with the Chicago orchestra without rehearsal, to stay the night in New York and go west by the afternoon train the next day. She telegraphed Chicago, but she did not telegraph Blasius, because she wished— the old fallacy of affection!—to "surprise" him. She could take it for granted that, at eleven on a cold winter night, he would be in the Tenth Street house and nowhere else in New York. She sent Poppas—paler than usual with accusing scorn—and her trunks on to Chicago, and with only her travelling bag and a sense of being very audacious in her behaviour and still very much in love, she took a cab for Tenth Street.

Since it was her intention to disturb Blasius as little as possible and to delight him as much as possible, she let herself in with her latch-key and went directly to his room. She did not find him there. Indeed, she found him where he should not have been at all. There must have been a trying scene.

Ruzenka was sent away in the morning, and the other two maids as well. By eight o'clock Cressida and Bouchalka had the house to themselves. Nobody had any breakfast. Cressida took the afternoon train to keep her engagement with Theodore Thomas, and to think over the situation. Blasius was left in the Tenth Street house with only the furnace man's wife to look after him. His explanation of his conduct was that he had been drinking too much. His digression, he swore, was casual. It had never occurred before, and he could only appeal to his wife's magnanimity. But it was, on the whole, easier for Cressida to be firm than to be yielding, and she knew herself too well to attempt a readjustment. She had never made shabby compromises, and it was too late for her to begin. When she returned to New York she went to a hotel, and she never saw Bouchalka alone again. Since he admitted her charge, the legal formalities were conducted so quietly that the granting of her divorce was announced in the morning papers before her friends knew that there was the least likelihood of one. Cressida's concert tours had interrupted the hospitalities of the house.

While the lawyers were arranging matters, Bouchalka came to see me. He was remorseful and miserable enough, and I think his perplexity was quite sincere. If there had been an intrigue with a woman of her own class, an infatuation, an affair, he said, he could understand. But anything so venial and accidental— He shook his head slowly back and forth. He assured me that he was not at all himself on that fateful evening, and that when he recovered himself he would have sent Ruzenka away, making proper provision for her, of course. It was an ugly thing, but ugly things sometimes happened in one's life, and one had to put them away and forget them. He could have overlooked any accident that might have occurred when his wife was on the road, with Poppas, for example. I cut him short, and he bent his head to my reproof.

"I know," he said, "such things are different with her. But when have I said that I am noble as she is? Never. But I have appreciated and I have adored. About me, say what you like. But if you say that in this there was any *méprise* to my wife, that is not true. I have lost all my place here. I came in from the streets; but I understand her, and all the fine things in her, better than any of you here. If that accident had not been, she would have lived happy with me for years. As for me, I have never believed in this happiness. I was not born under a good star. How did it come? By accident. It goes by accident. She tried to give good fortune to an unfortunate man, *un miserable;* that was her mistake. It cannot be done in this world. The lucky should marry the lucky." Bouchalka stopped and lit a cigarette. He sat sunk in my chair as if he never meant to get up again. His large hands, now so much plumper than when I first knew him, hung limp. When he had consumed his cigarette he turned to me again.

"I, too, have tried. Have I so much as written one note to a lady since she first put out her hand to help me? Some of the artists who sing my compositions have been quite willing to plague my wife a little if I make the least sign. With the Española, for instance, I have had to be very stern, *farouche;* she is so very playful. I have never given my wife the slightest annoyance of this kind. Since I married her, I have not kissed the cheek of one lady! Then one night I am bored and drink too much champagne and I become a fool. What does it matter? Did my wife marry the fool of me? No, she married me, with my mind and my feelings all here, as I am today. But she is getting a divorce from the fool of me, which she would never see *anyhow!* The stupidity which excuse me is the thing she will not overlook. Even in her memory of me she will be harsh."

His view of his conduct and its consequences was fatalistic: he was meant to have just so much misery every day of his life; for three years it had been withheld, had been piling up somewhere, underground, overhead; now the accumulation burst over him. He had come to pay his respects to me, he said, to declare his undying gratitude to Madame Garnet, and to bid me farewell. He took up his hat and cane and kissed my hand. I have never seen him since. Cressida made a settlement upon him, but even Poppas, tortured by envy and curiosity, never discovered how much it was. It was very little, she told me. "*Pour des gâteaux*," she added with a smile that was not unforgiving. She could not bear to think of his being in want when so little could make him comfortable.

He went back to his own village in Bohemia. He wrote her that the old monk, his teacher, was still alive, and that from the windows of his room in the town he could see the pigeons flying forth from and back to the monastery bell-tower all day long. He sent her a song, with his own words, about those pigeons,—quite a lovely thing.

He was the bell-tower, and *les colombes* were his memories of her.

IV

Jerome Brown proved, on the whole, the worst of Cressida's husbands, and, with the possible exception of her eldest brother, Buchanan Garnet, he was the most rapacious of the men with whom she had had to do. It was one thing to gratify every wish of a cake-loving fellow like Bouchalka, but quite another to stand behind a financier. And Brown would be a financier or nothing. After her marriage with him, Cressida grew rapidly older. For the first time in her life she wanted to go abroad and live—to get Jerome Brown away from the scene of his unsuccessful but undiscouraged activities. But Brown was not a man who could be amused and kept out of mischief in Continental hotels. He had to be a figure, if only a "mark," in Wall street. Nothing else would gratify his peculiar vanity. The deeper he went in, the more affectionately he told Cressida that now all her cares and anxieties were over. To try to get related facts out of his optimism was like trying to find frame work in a feather bed. All Cressida knew was that she was perpetually "investing" to save investments. When she told me she had put a mortgage on the Tenth Street house, her eyes filled with tears. "Why is it? I have never cared about money, except to make people happy with it, and it has been the curse of my life. It has spoiled all my relations with people. Fortunately," she added irrelevantly, drying her eyes, "Jerome and Poppas get along well." Jerome could have got along with anybody; that is a promoter's business. His warm hand, his flushed face, his bright eye, and his newest funny story,—Poppas had no weapons that could do execution with a man like that.

Though Brown's ventures never came home, there was nothing openly disastrous until the outbreak of the revolution in Mexico jeopardized his interests there. Then Cressida went to England—where she could always raise money from a faithful public—for a winter concert tour. When she sailed, her friends knew that her husband's affairs were in a bad way; but we did not know how bad until after Cressida's death.

Cressida Garnet, as all the world knows, was lost on the *Titanic*. Poppas and Horace, who had been travelling with her, were sent on a week earlier and came as safely to port as if they had never stepped out of their London hotel. But Cressida had waited for the first trip of the sea monster—she still believed that all advertising was good —and she went down on the road between the old world and the new. She had been ill, and when the collision occurred she was in her stateroom, a modest one somewhere down in the boat, for she was travelling economically. Apparently she never left her cabin. She was not seen on the decks, and none of the survivors brought any word of her.

On Monday, when the wireless messages were coming

from the *Carpathia* with the names of the passengers who had been saved, I went, with so many hundred others, down to the White Star offices. There I saw Cressida's motor, her redoubtable initials on the door, with four men sitting in the limousine. Jerome Brown, stripped of the promoter's joviality and looking flabby and old, sat behind with Buchanan Garnet, who had come on from Ohio. I had not seen him for years. He was now an old man, but he was still conscious of being in the public eye, and sat turning a cigar about in his face with that foolish look of importance which Cressida's achievement had stamped upon all the Garnets. Poppas was in front, with Horace. He was gnawing the finger of his chamois glove as it rested on the top of his cane. His head was sunk, his shoulders drawn together; he looked as old as Jewry. I watched them, wondering whether Cressida would come back to them if she could. After the last names were posted, the four men settled back into the powerful car— one of the best made—and the chauffeur backed off. I saw him dash away the tears from his face with the back of his driving glove. He was an Irish boy, and had been devoted to Cressida.

When the will was read, Henry Gilbert, the lawyer, an old friend of her early youth, and I, were named executors. A nice job we had of it. Most of her large fortune had been converted into stocks that were almost worthless. The marketable property realized only a hundred and fifty thousand dollars. To defeat the bequest of fifty thousand dollars to Poppas, Jerome Brown and her family contested the will. They brought Cressida's letters into court to prove that the will did not represent her intentions, often expressed in writing through many years, to "provide well" for them.

Such letters they were! The writing of a tired, overdriven woman; promising money, sending money herewith, asking for an acknowledgment of the draft sent last month, etc. In the letters to Jerome Brown she begged for information about his affairs and entreated him to go with her to some foreign city where they could live quietly and where she could rest; if they were careful, there would "be enough for all." Neither Brown nor her brothers and sisters had any sense of shame about these letters. It seemed never to occur to them that this golden stream, whether it rushed or whether it trickled, came out of the industry, out of the mortal body of a woman. They regarded her as a natural source of wealth; a copper vein, a diamond mine.

Henry Gilbert is a good lawyer himself, and he employed an able man to defend the will. We determined that in this crisis we would stand by Poppas, believing it would be Cressida's wish. Out of the lot of them, he was the only one who had helped her to make one penny of the money that had brought her so much misery. He was at least more deserving than the others. We saw to it that Poppas got his fifty thousand, and he actually departed, at last, for his city in *la sainte Asie*, where it never rains and where he will never again have to hold a hot water bottle to his face.

The rest of the property was fought for to a finish. Poppas out of the way, Horace and Brown and the Garnets quarrelled over her personal effects. They went from floor to floor of the Tenth Street house. The will provided that Cressida's jewels and furs and gowns were to go to her sisters. Georgie and Julia wrangled over them down to the last moleskin. They were deeply disappointed that some of the muffs and stoles which they remembered as very large, proved, when exhumed from storage and exhibited beside furs of a modern cut, to be ridiculously scant. A year ago the sisters were still reasoning with each other about pearls and opals and emeralds.

I wrote Poppas some account of these horrors, as during the court proceedings we had become rather better friends than of old. His reply arrived only a few days ago; a photograph of himself upon a camel, under which is written:

Traulich und Treu
ist's nur in der Tiefe:
falsch und feig
ist was dort oben sich freut!

His reply, and the memories it awakens—memories which have followed Poppas into the middle of Asia, seemingly,—prompted this informal narration.

A GOLD SLIPPER

A GOLD SLIPPER

Marshall McKann followed his wife and her friend Mrs. Post down the aisle and up the steps to the stage of the Carnegie Music Hall with an ill-concealed feeling of grievance. Heaven knew he never went to concerts, and to be mounted upon the stage in this fashion, as if he were a "highbrow" from Sewickley, or some unfortunate with a musical wife, was ludicrous. A man went to concerts when he was courting, while he was a junior partner. When he became a person of substance he stopped that sort of nonsense. His wife, too, was a sensible person, the daughter of an old Pittsburgh family as solid and well-rooted as the McKanns. She would never have bothered him about this concert had not the meddlesome Mrs. Post arrived to pay her a visit. Mrs. Post was an old school friend of Mrs. McKann, and because she lived in

Cincinnati she was always keeping up with the world and talking about things in which no one else was interested, music among them. She was an aggressive lady, with weighty opinions, and a deep voice like a jovial bassoon. She had arrived only last night, and at dinner she brought it out that she could on no account miss Kitty Ayrshire's recital; it was, she said, the sort of thing no one could afford to miss.

When McKann went into town in the morning he found that every seat in the music-hall was sold. He telephoned his wife to that effect, and, thinking he had settled the matter, made his reservation on the 11.25 train for New York. He was unable to get a drawing-room because this same Kitty Ayrshire had taken the last one. He had not intended going to New York until the following week, but he preferred to be absent during Mrs. Post's incumbency.

In the middle of the morning, when he was deep in his correspondence, his wife called him up to say the enterprising Mrs. Post had telephoned some musical friends in Sewickley and had found that two hundred folding-chairs were to be placed on the stage of the concert-hall, behind the piano, and that they would be on sale at noon. Would he please get seats in the front row? McKann asked if they would not excuse him, since he was going over to New York on the late train, would be tired, and would not have time to dress, etc. No, not at all. It would be foolish for two women to trail up to the stage unattended. Mrs. Post's husband always accompanied her to concerts, and she expected that much attention from her host. He needn't dress, and he could take a taxi from the concert-hall to the East Liberty station.

The outcome of it all was that, though his bag was at the station, here was McKann, in the worst possible humour, facing the large audience to which he was well known, and sitting among a lot of music students and excitable old maids. Only the desperately zealous or the morbidly curious would endure two hours in those wooden chairs, and he sat in the front row of this hectic body, somehow made a party to a transaction for which he had the utmost contempt.

When McKann had been in Paris, Kitty Ayrshire was singing at the Comique, and he wouldn't go to hear her —even there, where one found so little that was better to do. She was too much talked about, too much advertised; always being thrust in an American's face as if she were something to be proud of. Perfumes and petticoats and cutlets were named for her. Some one had pointed Kitty out to him one afternoon when she was driving in the Bois with a French composer—old enough, he judged, to be her father—who was said to be infatuated, carried away by her. McKann was told that this was one of the historic passions of old age. He had looked at her on that occasion, but she was so befrilled and befeathered that he caught nothing but a graceful outline and a small, dark head above a white ostrich boa. He had noted with disgust, however, the stooped shoulders and white imperial of the silk-hatted man beside her, and the senescent line of his back. McKann described to his wife this unpleasing picture only last night, while he was undressing, when he was making every possible effort to avert this concert party. But Bessie only looked superior and said she wished to hear Kitty Ayrshire sing, and that her "private life" was something in which she had no interest.

Well, here he was; hot and uncomfortable, in a chair much too small for him, with a row of blinding footlights glaring in his eyes. Suddenly the door at his right elbow opened. Their seats were at one end of the front row; he had thought they would be less conspicuous there than in the centre, and he had not forseeen that the singer would walk over him every time she came upon the stage. Her velvet train brushed against his trousers as she passed him. The applause which greeted her was neither overwhelming nor prolonged. Her conservative audience did not know exactly how to accept her toilette. They were accustomed to dignified concert gowns, like those which Pittsburgh matrons (in those days!) wore at their daughters' coming-out teas.

Kitty's gown that evening was really quite outrageous —the repartée of a conscienceless Parisian designer who took her hint that she wished something that would be entirely novel in the States. Today, after we have all of us, even in the uttermost provinces, been educated by Baskt and the various Ballets Russes, we would accept such a gown without distrust; but then it was a little disconcerting, even to the well-disposed. It was constructed of a yard or two of green velvet—a reviling, shrieking green which would have made a fright of any woman who had not inextinguishable beauty—and it was made without armholes, a device to which we were then so unaccustomed that it was nothing less than alarming. The velvet skirt split back from a transparent gold-lace petticoat, gold stockings, gold slippers. The narrow train was, apparently, looped to both ankles, and it kept curling about her feet like a serpent's tail, turning up its gold lining as if it were squirming over on its back. It was not, we felt, a costume in which to sing Mozart and Handel and Beethoven.

Kitty sensed the chill in the air, and it amused her. She liked to be thought a brilliant artist by other artists, but by the world at large she liked to be thought a daring creature. She had every reason to believe, from experience and from example, that to shock the great crowd was the surest way to get its money and to make her name a household word. Nobody ever became a household word of being an artist, surely; and you were not a thoroughly paying proposition until your name meant something on the sidewalk and in the barber-shop. Kitty studied her audience with an appraising eye. She liked the stimulus of this disapprobation. As she faced this hard-shelled public she felt keen and interested; she knew that she would give such a recital as cannot often be heard for money. She nodded gaily to the young man at the piano, fell into an attitude of seriousness, and began the group of Beethoven and Mozart songs.

Though McKann would not have admitted it, there were really a great many people in the concert-hall who knew what the prodigal daughter of their country was singing, and how well she was doing it. They thawed gradually under the beauty of her voice and the subtlety of her interpretation. She had sung seldom in concert then, and they had supposed her very dependent upon the accessories of the opera. Clean singing, finished artistry, were not what they expected from her. They began to feel, even, the wayward charm of her personality.

McKann, who stared coldly up at the balconies during her first song, during the second glanced cautiously at the green apparition before him. He was vexed with her for having retained a débutante figure. He comfortably classed all singers—especially operatic singers—as "fat Dutchwomen" or "shifty Sadies," and Kitty would not fit into his clever generalization. She displayed, under his nose, the only kind of figure he considered worth looking at—that of a very young girl, supple and sinuous and quick-silverish; thin, eager shoulders, polished white arms that were nowhere too fat and nowhere too thin. McKann found it agreeable to look at Kitty, but when he saw that the authoritative Mrs. Post, red as a turkey-cock with opinions she was bursting to impart, was studying and appraising the singer through her lorgnette, he gazed indifferently out into the house again. He felt for his watch, but his wife touched him warningly with her elbow—which, he noticed, was not at all like Kitty's.

When Miss Ayrshire finished her first group of songs, her audience expressed its approval positively, but guardedly. She smiled bewitchingly upon the people in front, glanced up at the balconies, and then turned to the company huddled on the stage behind her. After her gay and careless bows, she retreated toward the stage door. As she passed McKann, she again brushed lightly against him, and this time she paused long enough to glance down at him and murmur, "Pardon!"

In the moment her bright, curious eyes rested upon him, McKann seemed to see himself as if she were holding a mirror up before him. He beheld himself a heavy, solid figure, unsuitably clad for the time and place, with a florid, square face, well-visored with good living and sane opinions—an inexpressive countenance. Not a rock face, exactly, but a kind of pressed-brick-and-cement face, a "business" face upon which years and feelings had made no mark—in which cocktails might eventually blast out a few hollows. He had never seen himself so distinctly in his shaving-glass as he did in that instant when Kitty Ayrshire's liquid eye held him, when her bright, inquiring glance roamed over his person. After her prehensile train curled over his boot and she was gone, his wife turned to him and said in the tone of approbation one uses when an infant manifests its groping intelligence, "Very gracious of her, I'm sure!" Mrs. Post nodded oracularly. McKann grunted.

Kitty began her second number, a group of romantic German songs which were altogether more her affair than her first number. When she turned once to acknowledge the applause behind her, she caught McKann in the act of yawning behind his hand—he of course wore no gloves—and he thought she frowned a little. This did not embarrass him; it somehow made him feel important. When she retired after the second part of the program, she again looked him over curiously as she passed, and she took marked precaution that her dress did not touch him. Mrs. Post and his wife again commented upon her consideration.

The final number was made up of modern French songs which Kitty sang enchantingly, and at last her frigid public was thoroughly aroused. While she was coming back again and again to smile and curtsy, McKann whispered to his wife that if there were to be encores he had better make a dash for his train.

"Not at all," put in Mrs. Post. "Kitty is going on the same train. She sings in *Faust* at the opera tomorrow night, so she'll take no chances."

McKann once more told himself how sorry he felt for Post. At last Miss Ayrshire returned, escorted by her accompanist, and gave the people what she of course knew they wanted: the most popular aria from the French opera of which the title-rôle had become synonymous with her name—an opera written for her and to her and round about her, by the veteran French composer who adored her,—the last and not the palest flash of his creative fire. This brought her audience all the way. They clamoured for more of it, but she was not to be coerced. She had been unyielding through storms to which this was a summer breeze. She came on once more, shrugged her shoulders, blew them a kiss, and was gone. Her last smile was for that uncomfortable part of her audience seated behind her, and she looked with recognition at McKann and his ladies as she nodded good night to the wooden chairs.

McKann hurried his charges into the foyer by the nearest exit and put them into his motor. Then he went over to the Schenley to have a glass of beer and a rarebit before train-time. He had not, he admitted to himself, been so much bored as he pretended. The minx herself was well enough, but it was absurd in his fellow-townsmen to look owlish and uplifted about her. He had no rooted dislike for pretty women; he even didn't deny that gay girls had their place in the world, but they ought to be kept in their place. He was born a Presbyterian, just as he was born a McKann. He sat in his pew in the First Church every Sunday, and he never missed a presbytery meeting when he was in town. His religion was not very spiritual, certainly, but it was substantial and concrete, made up of good, hard convictions and opinions. It had something to do with citizenship, with whom one ought to marry, with the coal business (in which his own name was powerful), with the Republican party, and with all majorities and established precedents. He was hostile to fads, to enthusiasms, to individualism, to all changes except in mining machinery and in methods of transportation.

His equanimity restored by his lunch at the Schenley, McKann lit a big cigar, got into his taxi, and bowled off through the sleet.

There was not a sound to be heard or a light to be seen. The ice glittered on the pavement and on the naked trees. No restless feet were abroad. At eleven o'clock the rows of small, comfortable houses looked as empty of the troublesome bubble of life as the Allegheny cemetery itself. Suddenly the cab stopped, and McKann thrust his head out of the window. A woman was standing in the middle of the street addressing his driver in a tone of excitement. Over against the curb a lone electric stood despondent in the storm. The young woman, her cloak blowing about her, turned from the driver to McKann himself, speaking rapidly and somewhat incoherently.

"Could you not be so kind as to help us? It is Mees Ayrshire, the singer. The juice is gone out and we cannot move. We must get to the station. Mademoiselle cannot miss the train; she sings tomorrow night in New York. It is very important. Could you not take us to the station at East Liberty?"

McKann opened the door. "That's all right, but you'll

have to hurry. It's eleven-ten now. You've only got fifteen minutes to make the train. Tell her to come along."

The maid drew back and looked up at him in amazement. "But, the hand-luggage to carry, and Mademoiselle to walk! The street is like glass!"

McKann threw away his cigar and followed her. He stood silent by the door of the derelict, while the maid explained that she had found help. The driver had gone off somewhere to telephone for a car. Miss Ayrshire seemed not at all apprehensive; she had not doubted that a rescuer would be forthcoming. She moved deliberately; out of a whirl of skirts she thrust one fur-topped shoe— McKann saw the flash of the gold stocking above it— and alighted.

"So kind of you! So fortunate for us!" she murmured. One hand she placed upon his sleeve, and in the other she carried an armful of roses that had been sent up to the concert stage. The petals showered upon the sooty, sleety pavement as she picked her way along. They would be lying there tomorrow morning, and the children in those houses would wonder if there had been a funeral. The maid followed with two leather bags. As soon as he had lifted Kitty into his cab she exclaimed:

"My jewel-case! I have forgotten it. It is on the back seat, please. I am so careless!"

He dashed back, ran his hand along the cushions, and discovered a small leather bag. When he returned he found the maid and the luggage bestowed on the front seat, and a place left for him on the back seat beside Kitty and her flowers.

"Shall we be taking you far out of your way?" she asked sweetly. "I haven't an idea where the station is. I'm not even sure about the name. Céline thinks it is East Liberty, but I think it is West Liberty. An odd name, anyway. It is a Bohemian quarter, perhaps? A district where the law relaxes a trifle?"

McKann replied grimly that he didn't think the name referred to that kind of liberty.

"So much the better," sighed Kitty. "I am a Californian; that's the only part of America I know very well, and out there, when we called a place Liberty Hill or Liberty Hollow—well, we meant it. You will excuse me if I'm uncommunicative, won't you? I must not talk in this raw air. My throat is sensitive after a long program." She lay back in her corner and closed her eyes.

When the cab rolled down the incline at East Liberty station, the New York express was whistling in. A porter opened the door. McKann sprang out, gave him a claim check and his Pullman ticket, and told him to get his bag at the check-stand and rush it on that train.

Miss Ayrshire, having gathered up her flowers, put out her hand to take his arm. "Why, it's you!" she exclaimed, as she saw his face in the light. "What a coincidence!" She made no further move to alight, but sat smiling as if she had just seated herself in a drawing-room and were ready for talk and a cup of tea.

McKann caught her arm. "You must hurry, Miss Ayrshire, if you mean to catch that train. It stops here only a moment. Can you run?"

"Can I run!" she laughed. "Try me!"

As they raced through the tunnel and up the inside stairway, McKann admitted that he had never before made a dash with feet so quick and sure stepping out beside him. The white-furred boots chased each other like lambs at play, the gold stockings flashed like the spokes of a bicycle wheel in the sun. They reached the door of Miss Ayrshire's state-room just as the train began to pull out. McKann was ashamed of the way he was panting, for Kitty's breathing was as soft and regular as when she was reclining on the back seat of his taxi. It had somehow run in his head that all these stage women were a poor lot physically—unsound, overfed creatures, like canaries that are kept in a cage and stuffed with song-restorer. He retreated to escape her thanks. "Good night! Pleasant journey! Pleasant dreams!" With a friendly nod in Kitty's direction he closed the door behind him.

He was somewhat surprised to find his own bag, his Pullman ticket in the strap, on the seat just outside Kitty's door. But there was nothing strange about it. He had got the last section left on the train, No. 13, next the drawing-room. Every other berth in the car was made up. He was just starting to look for the porter when the door of the state-room opened and Kitty Ayrshire came out. She seated herself carelessly in the front seat beside his bag.

"Please talk to me a little," she said coaxingly. "I'm always wakeful after I sing, and I have to hunt some one to talk to. Céline and I get so tired of each other. We can speak very low, and we shall not disturb any one." She crossed her feet and rested her elbow on his Gladstone. Though she still wore her gold slippers and stockings, she did not, he thanked Heaven, have on her concert gown, but a very demure black velvet with some sort of pearl trimming about the neck. "Wasn't it funny," she proceeded, "that it happened to be you who picked me up? I wanted a word with you, anyway."

McKann smiled in a way that meant he wasn't being taken in. "Did you? We are not very old acquaintances."

"No, perhaps not. But you disapproved tonight, and I thought I was singing very well. You are very critical in such matters?"

He had been standing, but now he sat down. "My dear young lady, I am not critical at all. I know nothing about 'such matters.'"

"And care less?" she said for him. "Well, then we know where we are, in so far as that is concerned. What did displease you? My gown, perhaps? It may seem a little *outré* here, but it's the sort of thing all the imaginative designers abroad are doing. You like the English sort of concert gown better?"

"About gowns," said McKann, "I know even less than

about music. If I looked uncomfortable, it was probably because I was uncomfortable. The seats were bad and the lights were annoying."

Kitty looked up with solicitude. "I was sorry they sold those seats. I don't like to make people uncomfortable in any way. Did the lights give you a headache? They are very trying. They burn one's eyes out in the end, I believe." She paused and waved the porter away with a smile as he came toward them. Half-clad Pittsburghers were tramping up and down the aisle, casting sidelong glances at McKann and his companion. "How much better they look with all their clothes on," she murmured. Then, turning directly to McKann again: "I saw you were not well seated, but I felt something quite hostile and personal. You were displeased with me. Doubtless many people are, but I seldom get an opportunity to question them. It would be nice if you took the trouble to tell me why you were displeased."

She spoke frankly, pleasantly, without a shadow of challenge or hauteur. She did not seem to be angling for compliments. McKann settled himself in his seat. He thought he would try her out. She had come for it, and he would let her have it. He found, however, that it was harder to formulate the grounds of his disapproval than he would have supposed. Now that he sat face to face with her, now that she was leaning against his bag, he had no wish to hurt her.

"I'm a hard-headed business man," he said evasively,

"and I don't much believe in any of you fluffy-ruffles people. I have a sort of natural distrust of them all, the men more than the women."

She looked thoughtful. "Artists, you mean?" drawing her words slowly. "What is your business?"

"Coal."

"I don't feel any natural distrust of business men, and I know ever so many. I don't know any coal-men, but I think I could become very much interested in coal. Am I larger-minded than you?"

McKann laughed. "I don't think you know when you are interested or when you are not. I don't believe you know what it feels like to be really interested. There is so much fake about your profession. It's an affectation on both sides. I know a great many of the people who went to hear you tonight, and I know that most of them neither know nor care anything about music. They imagine they do, because it's supposed to be the proper thing."

Kitty sat upright and looked interested. She was certainly a lovely creature—the only one of her tribe he had ever seen that he would cross the street to see again. Those were remarkable eyes she had—curious, penetrating, restless, somewhat impudent, but not at all dulled by self-conceit.

"But isn't that so in everything?" she cried. "How many of your clerks are honest because of a fine, individual sense of honour? They are honest because it is the accepted rule of good conduct in business. Do you know"—she looked at him squarely—"I thought you would have something quite definite to say to me; but this is funny-paper stuff, the sort of objection I'd expect from your office-boy."

"Then you don't think it silly for a lot of people to get together and pretend to enjoy something they know nothing about?"

"Of course I think it silly, but that's the way God made audiences. Don't people go to church in exactly the same way? If there were a spiritual-pressure test-machine at the door, I suspect not many of you would get to your pews."

"How do you know I go to church?"

She shrugged her shoulders. "Oh, people with these old, ready-made opinions usually go to church. But you can't evade me like that." She tapped the edge of his seat with the toe of her gold slipper. "You sat there all evening, glaring at me as if you could eat me alive. Now I give you a chance to state your objections, and you merely criticize my audience. What is it? Is it merely that you happen to dislike my personality? In that case, of course, I won't press you."

"No," McKann frowned, "I perhaps dislike your professional personality. As I told you, I have a natural distrust of your variety."

"Natural, I wonder?" Kitty murmured. "I don't see why you should naturally dislike singers any more than

I naturally dislike coal-men. I don't classify people by their occupations. Doubtless I should find some coal-men repulsive, and you may find some singers so. But I have reason to believe that, at least, I'm one of the less repellent."

"I don't doubt it," McKann laughed, "and you're a shrewd woman to boot. But you are, all of you, according to my standards, light people. You're brilliant, some of you, but you've no depth."

Kitty seemed to assent, with a dive of her girlish head. "Well, it's a merit in some things to be heavy, and in others to be light. Some things are meant to go deep, and others to go high. Do you want all the women in the world to be profound?"

"You are all," he went on steadily, watching her with indulgence, "fed on hectic emotions. You are pampered. You don't help to carry the burdens of the world. You are self-indulgent and appetent."

"Yes, I am," she assented, with a candour which he did not expect. "Not all artists are, but I am. Why not? If I could once get a convincing statement as to why I should not be self-indulgent, I might change my ways. As for the burdens of the world—" Kitty rested her chin on her clasped hands and looked thoughtful. "One should give pleasure to others. My dear sir, granting that the great majority of people can't enjoy anything very keenly, you'll admit that I give pleasure to many more people than you do. One should help others who are less fortunate; at present I am supporting just eight people, besides those I hire. There was never another family in California that had so many cripples and hard-luckers as that into which I had the honour to be born. The only ones who could take care of themselves were ruined by the San Francisco earthquake some time ago. One should make personal sacrifices. I do; I give money and time and effort to talented students. Oh, I give something much more than that! something that you probably have never given to any one. I give, to the really gifted ones, my *wish*, my desire, my light, if I have any; and that, Mr. Worldly Wiseman, is like giving one's blood! It's the kind of thing you prudent people never give. That is what was in the box of precious ointment." Kitty threw off her fervour with a slight gesture, as if it were a scarf, and leaned back, tucking her slipper up on the edge of his seat. "If you saw the houses I keep up," she sighed, "and the people I employ, and the motor-cars I run— And, after all, I've only this to do it with." She indicated her slender person, which Marshall could almost have broken in two with his bare hands.

She was, he thought, very much like any other charming woman, except that she was more so. Her familiarity was natural and simple. She was at ease because she was not afraid of him or of herself, or of certain half-clad acquaintances of his who had been wandering up and down the car oftener than was necessary. Well, he was not afraid, either.

Kitty put her arms over her head and sighed again, feeling the smooth part in her black hair. Her head was small—capable of great agitation, like a bird's; or of great resignation, like a nun's. "I can't see why I shouldn't be self-indulgent, when I indulge others. I can't understand your equivocal scheme of ethics. Now I can understand Count Tolstoy's, perfectly. I had a long talk with him once, about his book 'What is Art?' As nearly as I could get it, he believes that we are a race who can exist only by gratifying appetites; the appetites are evil, and the existence they carry on is evil. We were always sad, he says, without knowing why; even in the Stone Age. In some miraculous way a divine ideal was disclosed to us, directly at variance with our appetites. It gave us a new craving, which we could only satisfy by starving all the other hungers in us. Happiness lies in ceasing to be and to cause being, because the thing revealed to us is dearer than any existence our appetites can ever get for us. I can understand that. It's something one often feels in art. It is even the subject of the greatest of all operas, which, because I can never hope to sing it, I love more than all the others." Kitty pulled herself up. "Perhaps you agree with Tolstoy?" she added languidly.

"No; I think he's a crank," said McKann, cheerfully.

"What do you mean by a crank?"

"I mean an extremist."

Kitty laughed. "Weighty word! You'll always have a

world full of people who keep to the golden mean. Why bother yourself about me and Tolstoy?"

"I don't, except when you bother me."

",Poor man! It's true this isn't your fault. Still, you did provoke it by glaring at me. Why did you go to the concert?"

"I was dragged."

"I might have known!" she chuckled, and shook her head. "No, you don't give me any good reasons. Your morality seems to me the compromise of cowardice, apologetic and sneaking. When righteousness becomes alive and burning, you hate it as much as you do beauty. You want a little of each in your life, perhaps—adulterated, sterilized, with the sting taken out. It's true enough they are both fearsome things when they get loose in the world; they don't, often."

McKann hated tall talk. "My views on women," he said slowly, "are simple."

"Doubtless," Kitty responded dryly, "but are they consistent? Do you apply them to your stenographers as well as to me? I take it for granted you have unmarried stenographers. Their position, economically, is the same as mine."

McKann studied the toe of her shoe. "With a woman, everything comes back to one thing." His manner was judicial.

She laughed indulgently. "So we are getting down to brass tacks, eh? I have beaten you in argument, and now you are leading trumps." She put her hands behind her head and her lips parted in a half-yawn. "Does everything come back to one thing? I wish I knew! It's more than likely that, under the same conditions, I should have been very like your stenographers—if they are good ones. Whatever I was, I would have been a good one. I think people are very much alike. You are more different than any one I have met for some time, but I know that there are a great many more at home like you. And even you —I believe there is a real creature down under these custom-made prejudices that save you the trouble of thinking. If you and I were shipwrecked on a desert island, I have no doubt that we would come to a simple and natural understanding. I'm neither a coward nor a shirk. You would find, if you had to undertake any enterprise of danger or difficulty with a woman, that there are several qualifications quite as important as the one to which you doubtless refer."

McKann felt nervously for his watch-chain. "Of course," he brought out, "I am not laying down any generalizations—" His brows wrinkled.

"Oh, aren't you?" murmured Kitty. "Then I totally misunderstood. But remember"— holding up a finger— "it is you, not I, who are afraid to pursue this subject further. Now, I'll tell you something." She leaned forward and clasped her slim, white hands about her velvet knee. "I am as much a victim of these ineradicable prejudices as you. Your stenographer seems to you a better sort. Well, she does to me. Just because her life is, presumably, greyer than mine, she seems better. My mind tells me that dulness, and a mediocre order of ability, and poverty, are not in themselves admirable things. Yet in my heart I always feel that the sales-women in shops and the working girls in factories are more meritorious than I. Many of them, with my opportunities, would be more selfish than I am. Some of them, with their own opportunities, are more selfish. Yet I make this senti-mental genuflection before the nun and the charwoman. Tell me, haven't you any weakness? Isn't there any fool-ish natural thing that unbends you a trifle and makes you feel gay?"

"I like to go fishing."

"To see how many fish you can catch?"

"No, I like the woods and the weather. I like to play a fish and work hard for him. I like the pussy-willows and the cold; and the sky, whether it's blue or grey—night coming on, every thing about it."

He spoke devoutly, and Kitty watched him through half-closed eyes. "And you like to feel that there are light-minded girls like me, who only care about the inside of shops and theatres and hotels, eh? You amuse me, you and your fish! But I mustn't keep you any longer. Haven't I given you every opportunity to state your case against me? I thought you would have more to say for yourself. Do you know, I believe it's not a case you have at all, but a grudge. I believe you are envious; that you'd like to be a tenor, and a perfect lady-killer!" She rose, smiling, and paused with her hand on the door of her state-room. "Anyhow, thank you for a pleasant evening. And, by the way, dream of me tonight, and not of either of those ladies who sat beside you. It does not matter much whom we live with in this world, but it matters a great deal whom we dream of." She noticed his bricky flush. "You are very naïf, after all, but, oh, so cautious! You are naturally afraid of everything new, just as I naturally want to try everything: new people, new religions—new miseries, even. If only there were more new things— If only you were really new! I might learn something. I'm like the Queen of Sheba—I'm not above learning. But you, my friend, would be afraid to try a new shaving soap. It isn't gravitation that holds the world in place; it's the lazy, obese cowardice of the people on it. All the same"—taking his hand and smiling encouragingly—"I'm going to haunt you a little. *Adios!*"

When Kitty entered her state-room, Céline, in her dressing-gown, was nodding by the window.

"Mademoiselle found the fat gentleman interesting?" she asked. "It is nearly one."

"Negatively interesting. His kind always say the same thing. If I could find one really intelligent man who held his views, I should adopt them."

"Monsieur did not look like an original," murmured Céline, as she began to take down her lady's hair.

* * *

McKann slept heavily, as usual, and the porter had to shake him in the morning. He sat up in his berth, and, after composing his hair with his fingers, began to hunt about for his clothes. As he put up the window-blind some bright object in the little hammock over his bed caught the sunlight and glittered. He stared and picked up a delicately turned gold slipper.

"Minx! hussy!" he ejaculated. "All that tall talk—! Probably got it from some man who hangs about; learned it off like a parrot. Did she poke this in here herself last night, or did she send that sneak-faced Frenchwoman? I like her nerve!" He wondered whether he might have been breathing audibly when the intruder thrust her head between his curtains. He was conscious that he did not look a Prince Charming in his sleep. He dressed as fast as he could, and, when he was ready to go to the washroom, glared at the slipper. If the porter should start to make up his berth in his absence— He caught the slipper, wrapped it in his pajama jacket, and thrust it into his bag. He escaped from the train without seeing his tormentor again.

Later McKann threw the slipper into the wastebasket in his room at the Knickerbocker, but the chambermaid, seeing that it was new and mateless, thought there must be a mistake, and placed it in his clothes-closet. He found it there when he returned from the theatre that evening. Considerably mellowed by food and drink and cheerful company, he took the slipper in his hand and decided to keep it as a reminder that absurd things could happen to people of the most clocklike deportment. When he got back to Pittsburgh, he stuck it in a lock-box in his vault, safe from prying clerks.

McKann has been ill for five years now, poor fellow! He still goes to the office, because it is the only place that interests him, but his partners do most of the work, and his clerks find him sadly changed—"morbid," they call his state of mind. He has had the pine-trees in his yard cut down because they remind him of cemeteries. On Sundays or holidays, when the office is empty, and he takes his will or his insurance-policies out of his lock-box, he often puts the tarnished gold slipper on his desk and looks at it. Somehow it suggests life to his tired mind, as his pine-trees suggested death—life and youth. When he drops over some day, his executors will be puzzled by the slipper.

As for Kitty Ayrshire, she has played so many jokes, practical and impractical, since then, that she has long ago forgotten the night when she threw away a slipper to be a thorn in the side of a just man.

SCANDAL

SCANDAL

Kitty Ayrshire had a cold, a persistent inflammation of the vocal cords which defied the throat specialist. Week after week her name was posted at the Opera, and week after week it was canceled, and the name of one of her rivals was substituted. For nearly two months she had been deprived of everything she liked, even of the people she liked, and had been shut up until she had come to hate the glass windows between her and the world, and the wintry stretch of the Park they looked out upon. She was losing a great deal of money, and, what was worse, she was losing life; days of which she wanted to make the utmost were slipping by, and nights which were to have crowned the days, nights of incalculable possibilities, were being stolen from her by women for whom she had no great affection. At first she had been courageous, but the strain of prolonged uncertainty was telling on her, and her nervous condition did not improve her larynx. Every morning Miles Creedon looked down her throat, only to put her off with evasions, to pronounce improvement that apparently never got her anywhere, to say that tomorrow he might be able to promise something definite.

Her illness, of course, gave rise to rumours—rumours that she had lost her voice, that at some time last summer she must have lost her discretion. Kitty herself was frightened by the way in which this cold hung on. She had had many sharp illnesses in her life, but always, before this, she had rallied quickly. Was she beginning to lose her resiliency? Was she, by any cursed chance, facing a bleak time when she would have to cherish herself? She protested, as she wandered about her sunny, many-windowed rooms on the tenth floor, that if she was going to have to live frugally, she wouldn't live at all. She wouldn't live on any terms but the very generous ones she had always known. She wasn't going to hoard her vitality. It must be there when she wanted it, be ready for any strain she chose to put upon it, let her play fast and loose with it; and then, if necessary, she would be ill for a while and pay the piper. But be systematically prudent and parsimonious she would not.

When she attempted to deliver all this to Doctor Creedon, he merely put his finger on her lips and said they would discuss these things when she could talk without injuring her throat. He allowed her to see no one except the Director of the Opera, who did not shine in conversation and was not apt to set Kitty going. The Director was a glum fellow, indeed, but during this calamitous time he had tried to be soothing, and he agreed with Creedon that she must not risk a premature appearance. Kitty was tormented by a suspicion that he was secretly backing the little Spanish woman who had sung many of her parts since she had been ill. He furthered the girl's interests because his wife had a very special consideration for her, and Madame had that consideration because— But that was too long and too dreary a story to follow out in one's mind. Kitty felt a tonsilitis disgust for opera-house politics, which, when she was in health, she rather enjoyed, being no mean strategist herself. The worst of being ill was that it made so many things and people look base.

She was always afraid of being disillusioned. She wished to believe that everything for sale in Vanity Fair was worth the advertised price. When she ceased to believe in these delights, she told herself, her pulling power would decline and she would go to pieces. In some way the chill of her disillusionment would quiver through the long, black line which reached from the box-office down to Seventh Avenue on nights when she sang. They shivered there in the rain and cold, all those people, because they loved to believe in her inextinguishable zest. She was no prouder of what she drew in the boxes than she was of that long, oscillating tail; little fellows in thin coats, Italians, Frenchmen, South-Americans, Japanese.

When she had been cloistered like a Trappist for six weeks, with nothing from the outside world but notes and flowers and disquieting morning papers, Kitty told Miles Creedon that she could not endure complete isolation any longer.

"I simply cannot live through the evenings. They have become horrors to me. Every night is the last night of a condemned man. I do nothing but cry, and that makes my throat worse."

Miles Creedon, handsomest of his profession, was better looking with some invalids than with others. His athletic figure, his red cheeks, and splendid teeth always had a cheering effect upon this particular patient, who hated anything weak or broken.

"What can I do, my dear? What do you wish? Shall I come and hold your lovely hand from eight to ten? You have only to suggest it."

"Would you do that, even? No, *caro mio*, I take far too much of your time as it is. For an age now you have been the only man in the world to me, and you have been charming! But the world is big, and I am missing it. Let some one come tonight, some one interesting, but not too interesting. Pierce Tevis, for instance. He is just back from Paris. Tell the nurse I may see him for an hour tonight," Kitty finished pleadingly, and put her fingers on the doctor's sleeve. He looked down at them and smiled whimsically.

Like other people, he was weak to Kitty Ayrshire. He would do for her things that he would do for no one else; would break any engagement, desert a dinner-table, leaving an empty place and an offended hostess, to sit all evening in Kitty's dressing-room, spraying her throat and calming her nerves, using every expedient to get her through a performance. He had studied her voice like a singing master; knew all of its idiosyncracies and the emotional and nervous perturbations which affected it. When it was permissible, sometimes when it was not permissible, he indulged her caprices. On this sunny morning her wan, disconsolate face moved him.

"Yes, you may see Tevis this evening if you will assure me that you will not shed one tear for twenty-four hours. I may depend on your word?" He rose, and stood before the deep couch on which his patient reclined. Her arch look seemed to say, "On what could you depend more?" Creedon smiled, and shook his head. "If I find you worse tomorrow—"

He crossed to the writing-table and began to separate a bunch of tiny flame-coloured rosebuds. "May I?" Selecting one, he sat down on the chair from which he had lately risen, and leaned forward while Kitty pinched the thorns from the stem and arranged the flower in his buttonhole.

"Thank you. I like to wear one of yours. Now I must

be off to the hospital. I've a nasty little operation to do this morning. I'm glad it's not you. Shall I telephone Tevis about this evening?"

Kitty hesitated. Her eyes ran rapidly about, seeking a likely pretext. Creedon laughed.

"Oh, I see. You've already asked him to come. You were so sure of me! Two hours in bed after lunch, with all the windows open, remember. Read something diverting, but not exciting; some homely British author; nothing *abandonné*. And don't make faces at me. Until tomorrow!"

When her charming doctor had disappeared through the doorway, Kitty fell back on her cushions and closed her eyes. Her mocking-bird, excited by the sunlight, was singing in his big gilt cage, and a white lilac-tree that had come that morning was giving out its faint sweetness in the warm room. But Kitty looked paler and wearier than when the doctor was with her. Even with him she rose to her part just a little; couldn't help it. And he took his share of her vivacity and sparkle, like every one else. He believed that his presence was soothing to her. But he admired; and whoever admired, blew on the flame, however lightly.

The mocking-bird was in great form this morning. He had the best bird-voice she had ever heard, and Kitty wished there were some way to note down his improvisations; but his intervals were not expressible in any scale she knew. Parker White had brought him to her, from

Ojo Caliente, in New Mexico, where he had been trained in the pine forests by an old Mexican and an ill-tempered, lame master-bird, half thrush, that taught young birds to sing. This morning, in his song there were flashes of silvery Southern springtime; they opened inviting roads of memory. In half an hour he had sung his disconsolate mistress to sleep.

That evening Kitty sat curled up on the deep couch before the fire, awaiting Pierce Tevis. Her costume was folds upon folds of diaphanous white over equally diaphanous rose, with a line of white fur about her neck. Her beautiful arms were bare. Her tiny Chinese slippers were embroidered so richly that they resembled the painted porcelain of old vases. She looked like a sultan's youngest, newest bride; a beautiful little toy-woman, sitting at one end of the long room which composed about her,— which, in the soft light, seemed happily arranged for her. There were flowers everywhere: rose-trees; camellia-bushes, red and white; the first forced hyacinths of the season; a feathery mimosa-tree, tall enough to stand under.

The long front of Kitty's study was all windows. At one end was the fireplace, before which she sat. At the other end, back in a lighted alcove, hung a big, warm, sympathetic interior by Lucien Simon,—a group of Kitty's friends having tea in the painter's salon in Paris. The room in the picture was flooded with early lamp-light, and one could feel the grey, chill winter twilight in the Paris streets outside. There stood the cavalier-like old composer, who had done much for Kitty, in his most characteristic attitude, before the hearth. Mme. Simon sat at the tea-table. B——, the historian, and H——, the philologist, stood in animated discussion behind the piano, while Mme. H—— was tying on the bonnet of her lovely little daughter. Marcel Durand, the physicist, sat alone in a corner, his startling black-and-white profile lowered broodingly, his cold hands locked over his sharp knee. A genial, red-bearded sculptor stood over him, about to touch him on the shoulder and waken him from his dream.

This painting made, as it were, another room; so that Kitty's study on Central Park West seemed to open into that charming French interior, into one of the most highly harmonized and richly associated rooms in Paris. There her friends sat or stood about, men distinguished, women at once plain and beautiful, with their furs and bonnets, their clothes that were so distinctly not smart— all held together by the warm lamp-light, by an indescribable atmosphere of graceful and gracious human living.

Pierce Tevis, after he had entered noiselessly and greeted Kitty, stood before her fire and looked over her shoulder at this picture.

"It's nice that you have them there together, now that they are scattered, God knows where, fighting to preserve just that. But your own room, too, is charming," he added at last, taking his eyes from the canvas.

Kitty shrugged her shoulders.

"Bah! I can help to feed the lamp, but I can't supply the dear things it shines upon."

"Well, tonight it shines upon you and me, and we aren't so bad." Tevis stepped forward and took her hand affectionately. "You've been over a rough bit of road. I'm so sorry. It's left you looking very lovely, though. Has it been very hard to get on?"

She brushed his hand gratefully against her cheek and nodded.

"Awfully dismal. Everything has been shut out from me but—gossip. That always gets in. Often I don't mind, but this time I have. People do tell such lies about me."

"Of course we do. That's part of our fun, one of the many pleasures you give us. It only shows how hard up we are for interesting public personages; for a royal family, for romantic fiction, if you will. But I never hear any stories that wound me, and I'm very sensitive about you."

"I'm gossiped about rather more than the others, am I not?"

"I believe! Heaven send that the day when you are not gossiped about is far distant! Do you want to bite off your nose to spite your pretty face? You are the sort of person who makes myths. You can't turn around without making one. That's your singular good luck. A whole staff of publicity men, working day and night, couldn't do for you what you do for yourself. There is an affinity between you and the popular imagination."

"I suppose so," said Kitty, and sighed. "All the same, I'm getting almost as tired of the person I'm supposed to be as of the person I really am. I wish you would invent a new Kitty Ayrshire for me, Pierce. Can't I do something revolutionary? Marry, for instance?"

Tevis rose in alarm.

"Whatever you do, don't try to change your legend. You have now the one that gives the greatest satisfaction to the greatest number of people. Don't disappoint your public. The popular imagination, to which you make such a direct appeal, for some reason wished you to have a son, so it has given you one. I've heard a dozen versions of the story, but it is always a son, never by any chance a daughter. Your public gives you what is best for you. Let well enough alone."

Kitty yawned and dropped back on her cushions.

"He still persists, does he, in spite of never being visible?"

"Oh, but he has been seen by ever so many people. Let me think a moment." He sank into an attitude of meditative ease. "The best description I ever had of him was from a friend of my mother, an elderly woman, thoroughly truthful and matter-of-fact. She has seen him often. He is kept in Russia, in St. Petersburg, that was. He is about eight years old and of marvellous beauty. He is always that in every version. My old friend has seen him being driven in his sledge on the Nevskii Prospekt on winter afternoons; black horses with silver bells and a giant in uniform on the seat beside the driver. He is always attended by this giant, who is responsible to the Grand Duke Paul for the boy. This lady can produce no evidence beyond his beauty and his splendid furs and the fact that all the Americans in Petrograd know he is your son."

Kitty laughed mournfully.

"If the Grand Duke Paul had a son, any old rag of a son, the province of Moscow couldn't contain him! He may, for aught I know, actually pretend to have a son. It would be very like him." She looked at her finger-tips and her rings disapprovingly for a moment. "Do you know, I've been thinking that I would rather like to lay hands on that youngster. I believe he'd be interesting. I'm bored with the world."

Tevis looked up and said quickly:

"Would you like him, really?"

"Of course I should," she said indignantly. "But, then, I like other things, too; and one has to choose. When one has only two or three things to choose from, life is hard; when one has many, it is harder still. No, on the whole, I don't mind that story. It's rather pretty, except for the Grand Duke. But not all of them are pretty."

"Well, none of them are very ugly; at least I never heard but one that troubled me, and that was long ago."

She looked interested.

"That is what I want to know; how do the ugly ones get started? How did that one get going and what was it about? Is it too dreadful to repeat?"

"No, it's not especially dreadful; merely rather shabby. If you really wish to know, and won't be vexed, I can tell you exactly how it got going, for I took the trouble to find out. But it's a long story, and you really had nothing whatever to do with it."

"Then who did have to do with it? Tell me; I should like to know exactly how even one of them originated."

"Will you be comfortable and quiet and not get into a rage, and let me look at you as much as I please?"

Kitty nodded, and Tevis sat watching her indolently while he debated how much of his story he ought not to tell her. Kitty liked being looked at by intelligent persons. She knew exactly how good looking she was; and she knew, too, that, pretty as she was, some of those rather sallow women in the Simon painting had a kind of beauty which she would never have. This knowledge, Tevis was thinking, this important realization, contributed more to her loveliness than any other thing about her; more than her smooth, ivory skin or her changing grey eyes, the delicate forehead above them, or even the dazzling smile, which was gradually becoming too bright and too intentional,—out in the world, at least. Here by her own fire she still had for her friends a smile less electric than the one she flashed from stages. She could still be, in short, *intime*, a quality which few artists keep, which few ever had.

Kitty broke in on her friend's meditations.

"You may smoke. I had rather you did. I hate to deprive people of things they like."

"No, thanks. May I have those chocolates on the teatable? They are quite as bad for me. May you? No, I suppose not." He settled himself by the fire, with the candy beside him, and began in the agreeable voice which always soothed his listener.

"As I said, it was a long while ago, when you first came back to this country and were singing at the Manhattan. I dropped in at the Metropolitan one evening to hear something new they were trying out. It was an off night, no pullers in the cast, and nobody in the boxes but governesses and poor relations. At the end of the first act two people entered one of the boxes in the second tier. The man was Siegmund Stein, the department-store millionaire, and the girl, so the men about me in the omnibus box began to whisper, was Kitty Ayrshire. I didn't know you then, but I was unwilling to believe that you were with Stein. I could not contradict them at that time, however, for the resemblance, if it was merely a resemblance, was absolute, and all the world knew that you were not singing at the Manhattan that night. The girl's hair was dressed just as you then wore yours. Moreover, her head was small and restless like yours, and she had your colouring, your eyes, your chin. She carried herself with the critical indifference one might expect in an artist who had come for a look at a new production that was clearly doomed to failure. She applauded lightly. She made comments to Stein when comments were natural enough. I thought, as I studied her face with the glass, that her nose was a trifle thinner than yours, a prettier nose, my dear Kitty, but stupider and more inflexible. All the same, I was troubled until I saw her laugh,— and then I knew she was a counterfeit. I had never seen you laugh, but I knew that you would not laugh like that. It was not boisterous; indeed, it was consciously re-fined,—mirthless, meaningless. In short, it was not the laugh of one whom our friends in there"—pointing to the Simon painting—"would honour with their affection and admiration."

Kitty rose on her elbow and burst out indignantly:

"So you would really have been hood-winked except for that! You may be sure that no woman, no intelligent woman, would have been. Why do we ever take the trouble to look like anything for any of you? I could count on my four fingers"—she held them up and shook them at him—"the men I've known who had the least perception of what any woman really looked like, and they were all dressmakers. Even painters"—glancing back in the direction of the Simon picture—"never get more than one type through their thick heads; they try to make all women look like some wife or mistress. You are all the same; you never see our real faces. What you

do see, is some cheap conception of prettiness you got
from a coloured supplement when you were adolescents.
It's too discouraging. I'd rather take vows and veil my
face for ever from such abominable eyes. In the kingdom
of the blind any petticoat is a queen." Kitty thumped the
cushion with her elbow. "Well, I can't do anything
about it. Go on with your story."

"Aren't you furious, Kitty! And I thought I was so
shrewd. I've quite forgotten where I was. Anyhow, I
was not the only man fooled. After the last curtain I met
Villard, the press man of that management, in the lobby,
and asked him whether Kitty Ayrshire was in the house.
He said he thought so. Stein had telephoned for a box,
and said he was bringing one of the artists from the other
company. Villard had been too busy about the new
production to go to the box, but he was quite sure the
woman was Ayrshire, whom he had met in Paris.

"Not long after that I met Dan Leland, a classmate of
mine, at the Harvard Club. He's a journalist, and he used
to keep such eccentric hours that I had not run across
him for a long time. We got to talking about modern
French music, and discovered that we both had a very
lively interest in Kitty Ayrshire.

" 'Could you tell me,' Dan asked abruptly, 'why, with
pretty much all the known world to choose her friends
from, this young woman should flit about with Siegmund
Stein? It prejudices people against her. He's a most ob-
jectionable person.'

" 'Have you,' I asked, 'seen her with him, yourself?,

"Yes, he had seen her driving with Stein, and some of the men on his paper had seen her dining with him at rather queer places down town. Stein was always hanging about the Manhattan on nights when Kitty sang. I told Dan that I suspected a masquerade. That interested him, and he said he thought he would look into the matter. In short, we both agreed to look into it. Finally, we got the story, though Dan could never use it, could never even hint at it, because Stein carries heavy advertising in his paper.

"To make you see the point, I must give you a little history of Siegmund Stein. Any one who has seen him never forgets him. He is one of the most hideous men in New York, but it's not at all the common sort of ugliness that comes from overeating and automobiles. He isn't one of the fat horrors. He has one of those rigid, horse-like faces that never tell anything; a long nose, flattened as if it had been tied down; a scornful chin; long, white teeth; flat cheeks, yellow as a Mongolian's; tiny, black eyes, with puffy lids and no lashes; dingy, dead-looking hair—looks as if it were glued on.

"Stein came here a beggar from somewhere in Austria. He began by working on the machines in old Rosenthal's garment factory. He became a speeder, a foreman, a salesman; worked his way ahead steadily until the hour when he rented an old dwelling-house on Seventh Avenue and began to make misses' and juniors' coats. I believe he was the first manufacturer to specialize in those particular articles. Dozens of garment manufacturers have come along the same road, but Stein is like none of the rest of them. He is, and always was, a personality. While he was still at the machine, a hideous, underfed little whippersnapper, he was already a youth of many-coloured ambitions, deeply concerned about his dress, his associates, his recreations. He haunted the old Astor Library and the Metropolitan Museum, learned something about pictures and porcelains, took singing lessons, though he had a voice like a crow's. When he sat down to his baked apple and doughnut in a basement lunch-room, he would prop a book up before him and address his food with as much leisure and ceremony as if he were dining at his club. He held himself at a distance from his fellow-workmen and somehow always managed to impress them with his superiority. He had inordinate vanity, and there are many stories about his foppishness. After his first promotion in Rosenthal's factory, he bought a new overcoat. A few days later, one of the men at the machines, which Stein had just quitted, appeared in a coat exactly like it. Stein could not discharge him, but he gave his own coat to a newly arrived Russian boy and got another. He was already magnificent.

"After he began to make headway with misses' and juniors' cloaks, he became a collector—etchings, china, old musical instruments. He had a dancing master, and engaged a beautiful Brazilian widow—she was said to be a secret agent for some South American republic—to teach him Spanish. He cultivated the society of the unknown great; poets, actors, musicians. He entertained them sumptuously, and they regarded him as a deep, mysterious Jew who had the secret of gold, which they had not. His business associates thought him a man of taste and culture, a patron of the arts, a credit to the garment trade.

"One of Stein's many ambitions was to be thought a success with women. He got considerable notoriety in the garment world by his attentions to an emotional actress who is now quite forgotten, but who had her little hour of expectation. Then there was a dancer; then, just after Gorky's visit here, a Russian anarchist woman. After that the coat-makers and shirtwaist-makers began to whisper that Stein's great success was with Kitty Ayrshire.

"It is the hardest thing in the world to disprove such a story, as Dan Leland and I discovered. We managed to worry down the girl's address through a taxi-cab driver who got next to Stein's chauffeur. She had an apartment in a decent-enough house on Waverly Place. Nobody ever came to see her but Stein, her sisters, and a little Italian girl from whom we got the story.

"The counterfeit's name was Ruby Mohr. She worked in a shirtwaist factory, and this Italian girl, Margarita, was her chum. Stein came to the factory when he was hunting for living models for his new department store. He looked the girls over, and picked Ruby out from several hundred. He had her call at his office after business hours, tried her out in cloaks and evening gowns, and offered her a position. She never, however, appeared as a model in the Sixth Avenue store. Her likeness to the newly arrived prima donna suggested to Stein another act in the play he was always putting on. He gave two of her sisters positions as saleswomen, but Ruby he established in an apartment on Waverly Place.

"To the outside world Stein became more mysterious in his behaviour than ever. He dropped his Bohemian friends. No more suppers and theatre-parties. Whenever Kitty sang, he was in his box at the Manhattan, usually alone, but not always. Sometimes he took two or three good customers, large buyers from St. Louis or Kansas City. His coat factory is still the biggest earner of his properties. I've seen him there with these buyers, and they carried themselves as if they were being let in on something; took possession of the box with a proprietory air, smiled and applauded and looked wise as if each and every one of them were friends of Kitty Ayrshire. While they buzzed and trained their field-glasses on the prima donna, Stein was impassive and silent. I don't imagine he even told many lies. He is the most insinuating cuss, anyhow. He probably dropped his voice or lifted his eyebrows when he invited them, and let their own eager imaginations do the rest. But what tales they took back to their provincial capitals!

"Sometimes, before they left New York, they were

lucky enough to see Kitty dining with their clever garment man at some restaurant, her back to the curious
crowd, her face half concealed by a veil or a fur collar.
Those people are like children; nothing that is true or
probable interests them. They want the old, gaudy lies,
told always in the same way. Siegmund Stein and Kitty
Ayrshire—a story like that, once launched, is repeated
unchallenged for years among New York factory sports.
In St. Paul, St. Jo, Sioux City, Council Bluffs, there used to
be clothing stores where a photograph of Kitty Ayrshire
hung in the fitting-room or over the proprietor's desk.

"This girl impersonated you successfully to the lower
manufacturing world of New York for two seasons. I
doubt if it could have been put across anywhere else in
the world except in this city, which pays you so magnifi-
cently and believes of you what it likes. Then you went
over to the Metropolitan, stopped living in hotels, took
this apartment, and began to know people. Stein dis-
continued his pantomime at the right moment, withdrew
his patronage. Ruby, of course, did not go back to shirt-
waists. A business friend of Stein's took her over, and
she dropped out of sight. Last winter, one cold, snowy
night, I saw her once again. She was going into a saloon
hotel with a tough-looking young fellow. She had been
drinking, she was shabby, and her blue shoes left stains
in the slush. But she still looked amazingly, convincingly
like a battered, hardened Kitty Ayrshire. As I saw her
going up the brass-edged stairs, I said to myself—"

"Never mind that." Kitty rose quickly, took an impatient step to the hearth, and thrust one shining porcelain slipper out to the fire. "The girl doesn't interest me. There is nothing I can do about her, and of course she never looked like me at all. But what did Stein do without me?"

"Stein? Oh, he chose a new rôle. He married with great magnificence—married a Miss Mandelbaum, a California heiress. Her people have a line of department stores along the Pacific Coast. The Steins now inhabit a great house on Fifth Avenue that used to belong to people of a very different sort. To old New-Yorkers, it's an historic house."

Kitty laughed, and sat down on the end of her couch nearest her guest; sat upright, without cushions.

"I imagine I know more about that house than you do. Let me tell you how I made the sequel to your story.

"It has to do with Peppo Amoretti. You may remember that I brought Peppo to this country, and brought him in, too, the year the war broke out, when it wasn't easy to get boys who hadn't done military service out of Italy. I had taken him to Munich to have some singing lessons. After the war came on we had to get from Munich to Naples in order to sail at all. We were told that we could take only hand luggage on the railways, but I took nine trunks and Peppo. I dressed Peppo in knickerbockers, made him brush his curls down over his ears like doughnuts, and carry a little violin-case. It took us eleven days to reach Naples. I got my trunks through purely by personal persuasion. Once at Naples, I had a frightful time getting Peppo on the boat. I declared him as hand-luggage; he was so travel-worn and so crushed by his absurd appearance that he did not look like much else. One inspector had a sense of humour, and passed him at that, but the other was inflexible. I had to be very dramatic. Peppo was frightened, and there is no fight in him, anyhow.

" '*Per me tutto e indifferente, Signorina*,' he kept whimpering. 'Why should I go without it? I have lost it.'

" 'Which?' I screamed. '*Not* the hat-trunk?'

" '*No, no; mia voce.* It is gone since Ravenna.'

"He thought he had lost his voice somewhere along the way. At last I told the inspector that I couldn't live without Peppo, and that I would throw myself into the bay. I took him into my confidence. Of course, when I found I had to play on that string, I wished I hadn't made the boy such a spectacle. But ridiculous as he was, I managed to make the inspector believe that I had kidnapped him, and that he was indispensable to my happiness. I found that incorruptible official, like most people, willing to aid one so utterly depraved. I could never have got that boy out for any proper, reasonable purpose, such as giving him a job or sending him to school. Well, it's a queer world! But I must cut all that and get to the Steins.

"That first winter Peppo had no chance at the Opera.

There was an iron ring about him, and my interest in him only made it all the more difficult. We've become a nest of intrigues down there; worse than the Scala. Peppo had to scratch along just any way. One evening he came to me and said he could get an engagement to sing for the grand rich Steins, but the condition was that I should sing with him. They would pay, oh, anything! And the fact that I had sung a private engagement with him would give him other engagements of the same sort. As you know, I never sing private engagements; but to help the boy along, I consented.

"On the night of the party, Peppo and I went to the house together in a taxi. My car was ailing. At the hour when the music was about to begin, the host and hostess appeared at my dressing-room, up-stairs. Isn't he wonderful? Your description was most inadequate. I never encountered such restrained, frozen, sculptured vanity. My hostess struck me as extremely good natured and jolly, though somewhat intimate in her manner. Her reassuring pats and smiles puzzled me at the time, I remember, when I didn't know that she had anything in particular to be large-minded and charitable about. Her husband made known his willingness to conduct me to the music-room, and we ceremoniously descended a staircase blooming like the hanging-gardens of Babylon. From there I had my first glimpse of the company. They *were* strange people. The women glittered like Christmas-trees. When we were half-way down the stairs, the buzz of conversation stopped so suddenly that some foolish remark I happened to be making rang out like oratory. Every face was lifted toward us. My host and I completed our descent and went the length of the drawing-room through a silence which somewhat awed me. I couldn't help wishing that one could ever get that kind of attention in a concert-hall. In the music-room Stein insisted upon arranging things for me. I must say that he was neither awkward nor stupid, not so wooden as most rich men who rent singers. I was properly affable. One has, under such circumstances, to be either gracious or pouty. Either you have to stand and sulk, like an old-fashioned German singer who wants the piano moved about for her like a tea-wagon, and the lights turned up and the lights turned down,—or you have to be a trifle forced, like a débutante trying to make good. The fixed attention of my audience affected me. I was aware of unusual interest, of a thoroughly enlisted public. When, however, my host at last left me, I felt the tension relax to such an extent that I wondered whether by any chance he, and not I, was the object of so much curiosity. But, at any rate, their cordiality pleased me so well that after Peppo and I had finished our numbers I sang an encore or two, and I stayed through Peppo's performance because I felt that they liked to look at me.

"I had asked not to be presented to people, but Mrs. Stein, of course, brought up a few friends. The throng began closing in upon me, glowing faces bore down from every direction, and I realized that, among people of such unscrupulous cordiality, I must look out for myself. I ran through the drawing-room and fled up the stairway, which was thronged with Old Testament characters. As I passed them, they all looked at me with delighted, cherishing eyes, as if I had at last come back to my native hamlet. At the top of the stairway a young man, who looked like a camel with its hair parted on the side, stopped me, seized my hands and said he must present himself, as he was such an old friend of Siegmund's bachelor days. I said, 'Yes, how interesting!' The atmosphere was somehow so thick and personal that I felt uncomfortable.

"When I reached my dressing-room Mrs. Stein followed me to say that I would, of course, come down to supper, as a special table had been prepared for me. I replied that it was not my custom.

" 'But here it is different. With us you must feel perfect freedom. Siegmund will never forgive me if you do not stay. After supper our car will take you home.' She was overpowering. She had the manner of an intimate and indulgent friend of long standing. She seemed to have come to make me a visit. I could only get rid of her by telling her that I must see Peppo at once, if she would be good enough to send him to me. She did not come back, and I began to fear that I would actually be dragged down to supper. It was as if I had been kidnapped. I felt like *Gulliver* among the giants. These people were all too—well, too much what they were. No chill of manner could hold them off. I was defenceless. I must get away. I ran to the top of the staircase and looked down. There was that fool Peppo, beleaguered by a bevy of fair women. They were simply looting him, and he was grinning like an idiot. I gathered up my train, ran down, and made a dash at him, yanked him out of that circle of rich contours, and dragged him by a limp cuff up the stairs after me. I told him that I must escape from that house at once. If he could get to the telephone, well and good; but if he couldn't get past so many deep-breathing ladies, then he must break out of the front door and hunt me a cab on foot. I felt as if I were about to be immured within a harem.

"He had scarcely dashed off when the host called my name several times outside the door. Then he knocked and walked in, uninvited. I told him that I would be inflexible about supper. He must make my excuses to his charming friends; any pretext he chose. He did not insist. He took up his stand by the fireplace and began to talk; said rather intelligent things. I did not drive him out; it was his own house, and he made himself agreeable. After a time a deputation of his friends came down the hall, somewhat boisterously, to say that supper could not be served until we came down. Stein was still standing by the mantel, I remember. He scattered them, without moving or speaking to them, by a portentous look. There is something hideously forceful about him. He took a very profound leave of me, and said he would order his car at once. In a moment Peppo arrived, splashed to the ankles, and we made our escape together.

"A week later Peppo came to me in a rage, with a paper called *The American Gentleman*, and showed me a page devoted to three photographs: Mr. and Mrs. Siegmund Stein, lately married in New York City, and Kitty Ayrshire, operatic soprano, who sang at their housewarming. Mrs. Stein and I were grinning our best, looked frantic with delight, and Siegmund frowned inscrutably between us. Poor Peppo wasn't mentioned. Stein has a publicity sense."

Tevis rose.

"And you have enormous publicity value and no discretion. It was just like you to fall for such a plot, Kitty. You'd be sure to."

"What's the use of discretion?" She murmured behind her hand. "If the Steins want to adopt you into their family circle, they'll get you in the end. That's why I don't feel compassionate about your Ruby. She and I are in the same boat. We are both the victims of circumstance, and in New York so many of the circumstances are Steins."

PAUL'S CASE

PAUL'S CASE

It was Paul's afternoon to appear before the faculty of the Pittsburgh High School to account for his various misdemeanours. He had been suspended a week ago, and his father had called at the Principal's office and confessed his perplexity about his son. Paul entered the faculty room suave and smiling. His clothes were a trifle outgrown, and the tan velvet on the collar of his open overcoat was frayed and worn; but for all that there was something of the dandy about him, and he wore an opal pin in his neatly knotted black four-in-hand, and a red carnation in his button-hole. This latter adornment the faculty somehow felt was not properly significant of the contrite spirit befitting a boy under the ban of suspension.

Paul was tall for his age and very thin, with high, cramped shoulders and a narrow chest. His eyes were remarkable for a certain hysterical brilliancy, and he continually used them in a conscious, theatrical sort of way, peculiarly offensive in a boy. The pupils were abnormally large, as though he were addicted to belladonna, but there was a glassy glitter about them which that drug does not produce.

When questioned by the Principal as to why he was there, Paul stated, politely enough, that he wanted to come back to school. This was a lie, but Paul was quite accustomed to lying; found it, indeed, indispensable for overcoming friction. His teachers were asked to state their respective charges against him, which they did with such a rancour and aggrievedness as evinced that this was not a usual case. Disorder and impertinence were among the offences named, yet each of his instructors felt that it was scarcely possible to put into words the real cause of the trouble, which lay in a sort of hysterically defiant manner of the boy's; in the contempt which they all knew he felt for them, and which he seemingly made not the least effort to conceal. Once, when he had been making a synopsis of a paragraph at the blackboard, his English teacher had stepped to his side and attempted to guide his hand. Paul had started back with a shudder and thrust his hands violently behind him. The astonished woman could scarcely have been more hurt and embarrassed had he struck at her. The insult was so involuntary and definitely personal as to be unforgettable. In one way and another, he had made all his teachers, men and women alike, conscious of the same feeling of physical aversion. In one class he habitually sat with his hand shading his eyes; in another he always looked out of the window during the recitation; in another he made a running commentary on the lecture, with humorous intent.

His teachers felt this afternoon that his whole attitude was symbolized by his shrug and his flippantly red carnation flower, and they fell upon him without mercy, his English teacher leading the pack. He stood through it smiling, his pale lips parted over his white teeth. (His lips were continually twitching, and he had a habit of raising his eyebrows that was contemptuous and irritating to the last degree.) Older boys than Paul had broken down and shed tears under that ordeal, but his set smile did not once desert him, and his only sign of discomfort was the nervous trembling of the fingers that toyed with the buttons of his overcoat, and an occasional jerking of the other hand which held his hat. Paul was always smiling, always glancing about him, seeming to feel that people might be watching him and trying to detect something. This conscious expression, since it was as far as possible from boyish mirthfulness, was usually attributed to insolence or "smartness."

As the inquisition proceeded, one of his instructors repeated an impertinent remark of the boy's, and the Principal asked him whether he thought that a courteous speech to make to a woman. Paul shrugged his shoulders slightly and his eyebrows twitched.

"I don't know," he replied. "I didn't mean to be polite or impolite, either. I guess it's a sort of way I have, of saying things regardless."

The Principal asked him whether he didn't think that a way it would be well to get rid of. Paul grinned and said he guessed so. When he was told that he could go, he bowed gracefully and went out. His bow was like a repetition of the scandalous red carnation.

His teachers were in despair, and his drawing master voiced the feeling of them all when he declared there was something about the boy which none of them understood. He added: "I don't really believe that smile of his comes altogether from insolence; there's something sort of haunted about it. The boy is not strong, for one thing. There is something wrong about `the fellow."

The drawing master had come to realize that, in looking at Paul, one saw only his white teeth and the forced animation of his eyes. One warm afternoon the boy had gone to sleep at his drawing-board, and his master had noted with amazement what a white, blue-veined face it was; drawn and wrinkled like an old man's about the eyes, the lips twitching even in his sleep.

His teachers left the building dissatisfied and unhappy; humiliated to have felt so vindictive toward a mere boy, to have uttered this feeling in cutting terms, and to have set each other on, as it were, in the grewsome game of intemperate reproach. One of them remembered having seen a miserable street cat set at bay by a ring of tormentors.

As for Paul, he ran down the hill whistling the Soldiers' Chorus from *Faust*, looking wildly behind him now and then to see whether some of his teachers were not there to witness his light-heartedness. As it was now late in the afternoon and Paul was on duty that evening as usher at Carnegie Hall, he decided that he would not go home to supper.

When he reached the concert hall the doors were not yet open. It was chilly outside, and he decided to go up into the picture gallery—always deserted at this hour —where there were some of Raffelli's gay studies of Paris streets and an airy blue Venetian scene or two that always exhilarated him. He was delighted to find no one in the gallery but the old guard, who sat in the corner, a newspaper on his knee, a black patch over one eye and the other closed. Paul possessed himself of the place and walked confidently up and down, whistling under his breath. After a while he sat down before a blue Rico and lost himself. When he bethought him to look at his watch, it was after seven o'clock, and he rose with a start and ran downstairs, making a face at Augustus Cæsar, peering out from the cast-room, and an evil gesture at the Venus of Milo as he passed her on the stairway.

When Paul reached the ushers' dressing-room half-a-dozen boys were there already, and he began excitedly to tumble into his uniform. It was one of the few that at all approached fitting, and Paul thought it very becoming —though he knew the tight, straight coat accentuated his narrow chest, about which he was exceedingly sensitive. He was always excited while he dressed, twanging all over to the tuning of the strings and the preliminary flourishes of the horns in the music-room; but tonight he seemed quite beside himself, and he teased and plagued the boys until, telling him that he was crazy, they put him down on the floor and sat on him.

Somewhat calmed by his suppression, Paul dashed out to the front of the house to seat the early comers. He was a model usher. Gracious and smiling he ran up and down the aisles. Nothing was too much trouble for him; he carried messages and brought programs as though it were his greatest pleasure in life, and all the people in his section thought him a charming boy, feeling that he remembered and admired them. As the house filled, he grew more and more vivacious and animated, and the colour came to his cheeks and lips. It was very much as though this were a great reception and Paul were the host. Just as the musicians came out to take their places, his English teacher arrived with checks for the seats which a prominent manufacturer had taken for the season. She betrayed some embarrassment when she handed Paul the tickets, and a *hauteur* which subsequently made her feel very foolish. Paul was startled for a moment, and had the feeling of wanting to put her out; what business

had she here among all these fine people and gay colours?
He looked her over and decided that she was not appro-
priately dressed and must be a fool to sit downstairs in
such togs. The tickets had probably been sent her out of
kindness, he reflected, as he put down a seat for her,
and she had about as much right to sit there as he had.

When the symphony began Paul sank into one of the
rear seats with a long sigh of relief, and lost himself as
he had done before the Rico. It was not that symphonies,
as such, meant anything in particular to Paul, but the
first sigh of the instruments seemed to free some hilarious
spirit within him; something that struggled there like the
Genius in the bottle found by the Arab fisherman. He
felt a sudden zest of life; the lights danced before his eyes
and the concert hall blazed into unimaginable splendour.
When the soprano soloist came on, Paul forgot even the
nastiness of his teacher's being there, and gave himself up
to the peculiar intoxication such personages always had
for him. The soloist chanced to be a German woman,
by no means in her first youth, and the mother of many
children; but she wore a satin gown and a tiara, and she
had that indefinable air of achievement, that world-shine
upon her, which always blinded Paul to any possible de-
fects.

After a concert was over, Paul was often irritable and
wretched until he got to sleep,—and tonight he was even
more than usually restless. He had the feeling of not
being able to let down; of its being impossible to give up

this delicious excitement which was the only thing that could be called living at all. During the last number he withdrew and, after hastily changing his clothes in the dressing-room, slipped out to the side door where the singer's carriage stood. Here he began pacing rapidly up and down the walk, waiting to see her come out.

Over yonder the Schenley, in its vacant stretch, loomed big and square through the fine rain, the windows of its twelve stories glowing like those of a lighted card-board house under a Christmas tree. All the actors and singers of any importance stayed there when they were in the city, and a number of the big manufacturers of the place lived there in the winter. Paul had often hung about the hotel, watching the people go in and out, longing to enter and leave school-masters and dull care behind him for ever.

At last the singer came out, accompanied by the conductor, who helped her into her carriage and closed the door with a cordial *auf wiedersehen*,—which set Paul to wondering whether she were not an old sweetheart of his. Paul followed the carriage over to the hotel, walking so rapidly as not to be far from the entrance when the singer alighted and disappeared behind the swinging glass doors which were opened by a negro in a tall hat and a long coat. In the moment that the door was ajar, it seemed to Paul that he, too, entered. He seemed to feel himself go after her up the steps, into the warm, lighted building, into an exotic, a tropical world of shiny, glistening surfaces and basking ease. He reflected upon the mysterious dishes that were brought into the dining-room, the green bottles in buckets of ice, as he had seen them in the supper party pictures of the Sunday supplement. A quick gust of wind brought the rain down with sudden vehemence, and Paul was startled to find that he was still outside in the slush of the gravel driveway; that his boots were letting in the water and his scanty overcoat was clinging wet about him; that the lights in front of the concert hall were out, and that the rain was driving in sheets between him and the orange glow of the windows above him. There it was, what he wanted—tangibly before him, like the fairy world of a Christmas pantomime; as the rain beat in his face, Paul wondered whether he were destined always to shiver in the black night outside, looking up at it.

He turned and walked reluctantly toward the car tracks. The end had to come sometime; his father in his night-clothes at the top of the stairs, explanations that did not explain, hastily improvised fictions that were forever tripping him up, his upstairs room and its horrible yellow wallpaper, the creaking bureau with the greasy plush collar-box, and over his painted wooden bed the pictures of George Washington and John Calvin, and the framed motto, "Feed my Lambs," which had been worked in red worsted by his mother, whom Paul could not remember.

Half an hour later, Paul alighted from the Negley

Avenue car and went slowly down one of the side streets off the main thoroughfare. It was a highly respectable street, where all the houses were exactly alike, and where business men of moderate means begot and reared large families of children, all of whom went to Sabbath-school and learned the shorter catechism, and were interested in arithmetic; all of whom were as exactly alike as their homes, and of a piece with the monotony in which they lived. Paul never went up Cordelia Street without a shudder of loathing. His home was next the house of the Cumberland minister. He approached it tonight with the nerveless sense of defeat, the hopeless feeling of sinking back forever into ugliness and commonness that he had always had when he came home. The moment he turned into Cordelia Street he felt the waters close above his head. After each of these orgies of living, he experienced all the physical depression which follows a debauch; the loathing of respectable beds, of common food, of a house permeated by kitchen odours; a shuddering repulsion for the flavourless, colourless mass of every-day existence; a morbid desire for cool things and soft lights and fresh flowers.

The nearer he approached the house, the more absolutely unequal Paul felt to the sight of it all; his ugly sleeping chamber; the cold bath-room with the grimy zinc tub, the cracked mirror, the dripping spiggots; his father, at the top of the stairs, his hairy legs sticking out from his nightshirt, his feet thrust into carpet slippers.

He was so much later than usual that there would certainly be inquiries and reproaches. Paul stopped short before the door. He felt that he could not be accosted by his father tonight; that he could not toss again on that miserable bed. He would not go in. He would tell his father that he had no car fare, and it was raining so hard he had gone home with one of the boys and stayed all night.

Meanwhile, he was wet and cold. He went around to the back of the house and tried one of the basement windows, found it open, raised it cautiously, and scrambled down the cellar wall to the floor. There he stood, holding his breath, terrified by the noise he had made; but the floor above him was silent, and there was no creak on the stairs. He found a soap-box, and carried it over to the soft ring of light that streamed from the furnace door, and sat down. He was horribly afraid of rats, so he did not try to sleep, but sat looking distrustfully at the dark, still terrified lest he might have awakened his father. In such reactions, after one of the experiences which made days and nights out of the dreary blanks of the calendar, when his senses were deadened, Paul's head was always singularly clear. Suppose his father had heard him getting in at the window and had come down and shot him for a burglar? Then, again, suppose his father had come down, pistol in hand, and he had cried out in time to save himself, and his father had been horrified to think how nearly he had killed him? Then, again, suppose a day should come when his father would remember that night, and wish there had been no warning cry to stay his hand? With this last supposition Paul entertained himself until daybreak.

The following Sunday was fine; the sodden November chill was broken by the last flash of autumnal summer. In the morning Paul had to go to church and Sabbath-school, as always. On seasonable Sunday afternoons the burghers of Cordelia Street usually sat out on their front "stoops," and talked to their neighbours on the next stoop, or called to those across the street in neighbourly fashion. The men sat placidly on gay cushions placed upon the steps that led down to the sidewalk, while the women, in their Sunday "waists," sat in rockers on the cramped porches, pretending to be greatly at their ease. The children played in the streets; there were so many of them that the place resembled the recreation grounds of a kindergarten. The men on the steps—all in their shirt sleeves, their vests unbuttoned—sat with their legs well apart, their stomachs comfortably protruding, and talked of the prices of things, or told anecdotes of the sagacity of their various chiefs and overlords. They occasionally looked over the multitude of squabbling children, listened affectionately to their high-pitched, nasal voices, smiling to see their own proclivities reproduced in their offspring, and interspersed their legends of the iron kings with remarks about their sons' progress at school, their grades in arithmetic, and the amounts they had saved in their toy banks.

On this last Sunday of November, Paul sat all the afternoon on the lowest step of his "stoop," staring into the street, while his sisters, in their rockers, were talking to the minister's daughters next door about how many shirt-waists they had made in the last week, and how many waffles some one had eaten at the last church supper. When the weather was warm, and his father was in a particularly jovial frame of mind, the girls made lemonade, which was always brought out in a red-glass pitcher, ornamented with forget-me-nots in blue enamel. This the girls thought very fine, and the neighbours joked about the suspicious colour of the pitcher.

Today Paul's father, on the top step, was talking to a young man who shifted a restless baby from knee to knee. He happened to be the young man who was daily held up to Paul as a model, and after whom it was his father's dearest hope that he would pattern. This young man was of a ruddy complexion, with a compressed, red mouth, and faded, near-sighted eyes, over which he wore thick spectacles, with gold bows that curved about his ears. He was clerk to one of the magnates of a great steel corporation, and was looked upon in Cordelia Street as a young man with a future. There was a story that, some five years ago—he was now barely twenty-six—he had been a trifle "dissipated," but in order to curb his appetites and save the loss of time and strength that a sowing of wild oats might have entailed, he had taken his chief's advice, oft reiterated to his employés, and at twenty-one had married the first woman whom he could persuade to share his fortunes. She happened to be an angular school-mistress, much older than he, who also wore thick glasses, and who had now borne him four children, all near-sighted, like herself.

The young man was relating how his chief, now cruising in the Mediterranean, kept in touch with all the details of the business, arranging his office hours on his yacht just as though he were at home, and "knocking off work enough to keep two stenographers busy." His father told, in turn, the plan his corporation was considering, of putting in an electric railway plant at Cairo. Paul snapped his teeth; he had an awful apprehension that they might spoil it all before he got there. Yet he rather liked to hear these legends of the iron kings, that were told and retold on Sundays and holidays; these stories of palaces in Venice, yachts on the Mediterranean, and high play at Monte Carlo appealed to his fancy, and he was interested in the triumphs of cash boys who had become famous, though he had no mind for the cash-boy stage.

After supper was over, and he had helped to dry the dishes, Paul nervously asked his father whether he could go to George's to get some help in his geometry, and still more nervously asked for car-fare. This latter request he had to repeat, as his father, on principle, did not like to hear requests for money, whether much or little. He asked Paul whether he could not go to some boy who lived nearer, and told him that he ought not to leave his school work until Sunday; but he gave him the dime. He was not a poor man, but he had a worthy ambition to come up in the world. His only reason for allowing Paul to usher was that he thought a boy ought to be earning a little.

Paul bounded upstairs, scrubbed the greasy odour of the dish-water from his hands with the ill-smelling soap he hated, and then shook over his fingers a few drops of violet water from the bottle he kept hidden in his drawer. He left the house with his geometry conspicuously under his arm, and the moment he got out of Cordelia Street and boarded a downtown car, he shook off the lethargy of two deadening days, and began to live again.

The leading juvenile of the permanent stock company which played at one of the downtown theatres was an acquaintance of Paul's, and the boy had been invited to drop in at the Sunday-night rehearsals whenever he could. For more than a year Paul had spent every available moment loitering about Charley Edwards's dressing-room. He had won a place among Edwards's following not only because the young actor, who could not afford to employ a dresser, often found him useful, but because he recognized in Paul something akin to what churchmen term "vocation."

It was at the theatre and at Carnegie Hall that Paul really lived; the rest was but a sleep and a forgetting. This was Paul's fairy tale, and it had for him all the allurement of a secret love. The moment he inhaled the gassy, painty, dusty odour behind the scenes, he breathed like a prisoner set free, and felt within him the possibility of doing or saying splendid, brilliant things. The moment the cracked orchestra beat out the overture from *Martha*, or jerked at the serenade from *Rigoletto*, all stupid and ugly things slid from him, and his senses were deliciously, yet delicately fired.

Perhaps it was because, in Paul's world, the natural nearly always wore the guise of ugliness, that a certain element of artificiality seemed to him necessary in beauty. Perhaps it was because his experience of life elsewhere was so full of Sabbath-school picnics, petty economies, wholesome advice as to how to succeed in life, and the unescapable odours of cooking, that he found this existence so alluring, these smartly-clad men and women so attractive, that he was so moved by these starry apple orchards that bloomed perennially under the lime-light.

It would be difficult to put it strongly enough how convincingly the stage entrance of that theatre was for Paul the actual portal of Romance. Certainly none of the company ever suspected it, least of all Charley Edwards. It was very like the old stories that used to float about London of fabulously rich Jews, who had subterranean halls, with palms, and fountains, and soft lamps and richly apparelled women who never saw the disenchanting light of London day. So, in the midst of that smoke-palled city, enamoured of figures and grimy toil, Paul had his secret temple, his wishing-carpet, his bit of blue-and-white Mediterranean shore bathed in perpetual sunshine.

Several of Paul's teachers had a theory that his imagination had been perverted by garish fiction; but the truth was, he scarcely ever read at all. The books at home were not such as would either tempt or corrupt a youthful mind, and as for reading the novels that some of his friends urged upon him—well, he got what he wanted much more quickly from music; any sort of music, from an orchestra to a barrel organ. He needed only the spark, the indescribable thrill that made his imagination master of his senses, and he could make plots and pictures enough of his own. It was equally true that he was not stage-struck—not, at any rate, in the usual acceptation of that expression. He had no desire to become an actor, any more than he had to become a musician. He felt no necessity to do any of these things; what he wanted was to see, to be in the atmosphere, float on the wave of it, to be carried out, blue league after blue league, away from everything.

After a night behind the scenes, Paul found the school-room more than ever repulsive; the bare floors and naked walls; the prosy men who never wore frock coats, or violets in their buttonholes; the women with their dull gowns, shrill voices, and pitiful seriousness about prepositions that govern the dative. He could not bear to have the other pupils think, for a moment, that he took these people seriously; he must convey to them that he considered it all trivial, and was there only by way of a joke, anyway. He had autograph pictures of all the members of the stock company which he showed his classmates, telling them the most incredible stories of his familiarity with these people, of his acquaintance with the soloists who came to Carnegie Hall, his suppers with them and the flowers he sent them. When these stories lost their effect, and his audience grew listless, he would bid all the boys good-bye, announcing that he was going to travel for awhile; going to Naples, to California, to Egypt. Then, next Monday, he would slip back, conscious and nervously smiling; his sister was ill, and he would have to defer his voyage until spring.

Matters went steadily worse with Paul at school. In the itch to let his instructors know how heartily he despised them, and how thoroughly he was appreciated elsewhere, he mentioned once or twice that he had no time to fool with theorems; adding—with a twitch of the eyebrows and a touch of that nervous bravado which so perplexed them—that he was helping the people down at the stock company; they were old friends of his.

The upshot of the matter was, that the Principal went to Paul's father, and Paul was taken out of school and put to work. The manager at Carnegie Hall was told to get another usher in his stead; the doorkeeper at the theatre was warned not to admit him to the house; and Charley Edwards remorsefully promised the boy's father not to see him again.

The members of the stock company were vastly amused when some of Paul's stories reached them—especially the women. They were hard-working women, most of them supporting indolent husbands or brothers, and they laughed rather bitterly at having stirred the boy to such fervid and florid inventions. They agreed with the faculty and with his father, that Paul's was a bad case.

The east-bound train was ploughing through a January snow-storm; the dull dawn was beginning to show grey when the engine whistled a mile out of Newark. Paul started up from the seat where he had lain curled in uneasy slumber, rubbed the breath-misted window glass with his hand, and peered out. The snow was whirling in curling eddies above the white bottom lands, and the drifts lay already deep in the fields and along the fences, while here and there the long dead grass and dried weed stalks protruded black above it. Lights shone from the scattered houses, and a gang of labourers who stood beside the track waved their lanterns.

Paul had slept very little, and he felt grimy and un-comfortable. He had made the all-night journey in a day coach because he was afraid if he took a Pullman he might be seen by some Pittsburgh business man who had noticed him in Denny & Carson's office. When the whistle woke him, he clutched quickly at his breast pocket, glancing about him with an uncertain smile. But the little, clay-bespattered Italians were still sleeping, the slatternly women across the aisle were in open-mouthed oblivion, and even the crumby, crying babies were for the nonce stilled. Paul settled back to struggle with his impatience as best he could.

When he arrived at the Jersey City station, he hurried through his breakfast, manifestly ill at ease and keeping a sharp eye about him. After he reached the Twenty-third Street station, he consulted a cabman, and had himself driven to a men's furnishing establishment which was just opening for the day. He spent upward of two hours there, buying with endless reconsidering and great care. His new street suit he put on in the fitting-room; the frock coat and dress clothes he had bundled into the cab with his new shirts. Then he drove to a hatter's and a shoe house. His next errand was at Tiffany's, where he selected silver mounted brushes and a scarf-pin. He would not wait to have his silver marked, he said. Lastly, he stopped at a trunk shop on Broadway, and had his purchases packed into various travelling bags.

It was a little after one o'clock when he drove up to the Waldorf, and, after settling with the cabman, went into the office. He registered from Washington; said his mother and father had been abroad, and that he had come down to await the arrival of their steamer. He told his story plausibly and had no trouble, since he offered to pay for them in advance, in engaging his rooms; a sleeping-room, sitting-room and bath.

Not once, but a hundred times Paul had planned this

entry into New York. He had gone over every detail of it with Charley Edwards, and in his scrap book at home there were pages of description about New York hotels, cut from the Sunday papers.

When he was shown to his sitting-room on the eighth floor, he saw at a glance that everything was as it should be; there was but one detail in his mental picture that the place did not realize, so he rang for the bell boy and sent him down for flowers. He moved about nervously until the boy returned, putting away his new linen and fingering it delightedly as he did so. When the flowers came, he put them hastily into water, and then tumbled into a hot bath. Presently he came out of his white bath-room, resplendent in his new silk underwear, and playing with the tassels of his red robe. The snow was whirling so fiercely outside his windows that he could scarcely see across the street; but within, the air was deliciously soft and fragrant. He put the violets and jonquils on the tabouret beside the couch, and threw himself down with a long sigh, covering himself with a Roman blanket. He was thoroughly tired; he had been in such haste, he had stood up to such a strain, covered so much ground in the last twenty-four hours, that he wanted to think how it had all come about. Lulled by the sound of the wind, the warm air, and the cool fragrance of the flowers, he sank into deep, drowsy retrospection.

It had been wonderfully simple; when they had shut him out of the theatre and concert hall, when they had taken away his bone, the whole thing was virtually determined. The rest was a mere matter of opportunity. The only thing that at all surprised him was his own courage—for he realized well enough that he had always been tormented by fear, a sort of apprehensive dread that, of late years, as the meshes of the lies he had told closed about him, had been pulling the muscles of his body tighter and tighter. Until now, he could not remember a time when he had not been dreading something. Even when he was a little boy, it was always there—behind him, or before, or on either side. There had always been the shadowed corner, the dark place into which he dared not look, but from which something seemed always to be watching him—and Paul had done things that were not pretty to watch, he knew.

But now he had a curious sense of relief, as though he had at last thrown down the gauntlet to the thing in the corner.

Yet it was but a day since he had been sulking in the traces; but yesterday afternoon that he had been sent to the bank with Denny & Carson's deposit, as usual—but this time he was instructed to leave the book to be balanced. There was above two thousand dollars in checks, and nearly a thousand in the bank notes which he had taken from the book and quietly transferred to his pocket. At the bank he had made out a new deposit slip. His nerves had been steady enough to permit of his returning to the office, where he had finished his work and asked for a full day's holiday tomorrow, Saturday, giving a perfectly reasonable pretext. The bank book, he knew, would not be returned before Monday or Tuesday, and his father would be out of town for the next week. From the time he slipped the bank notes into his pocket until he boarded the night train for New York, he had not known a moment's hesitation.

How astonishingly easy it had all been; here he was, the thing done; and this time there would be no awakening, no figure at the top of the stairs. He watched the snow flakes whirling by his window until he fell asleep.

When he awoke, it was four o'clock in the afternoon. He bounded up with a start; one of his precious days gone already! He spent nearly an hour in dressing, watching every stage of his toilet carefully in the mirror. Everything was quite perfect; he was exactly the kind of boy he had always wanted to be.

When he went downstairs, Paul took a carriage and drove up Fifth avenue toward the Park. The snow had somewhat abated; carriages and tradesmen's wagons were hurrying soundlessly to and fro in the winter twilight; boys in woollen mufflers were shovelling off the doorsteps; the avenue stages made fine spots of colour against the white street. Here and there on the corners whole flower gardens blooming behind glass windows, against which the snow flakes stuck and melted; violets, roses, carnations, lilies of the valley—somehow vastly more lovely and alluring that they blossomed thus unnaturally in the snow. The Park itself was a wonderful stage winter-piece.

When he returned, the pause of the twilight had ceased, and the tune of the streets had changed. The snow was falling faster, lights streamed from the hotels that reared their many stories fearlessly up into the storm, defying the raging Atlantic winds. A long, black stream of carriages poured down the avenue, intersected here and there by other streams, tending horizontally. There were a score of cabs about the entrance of his hotel, and his driver had to wait. Boys in livery were running in and out of the awning stretched across the sidewalk, up and down the red velvet carpet laid from the door to the street. Above, about, within it all, was the rumble and roar, the hurry and toss of thousands of human beings as hot for pleasure as himself, and on every side of him towered the glaring affirmation of the omnipotence of wealth.

The boy set his teeth and drew his shoulders together in a spasm of realization; the plot of all dramas, the text of all romances, the nerve-stuff of all sensations was whirling about him like the snow flakes. He burnt like a faggot in a tempest.

When Paul came down to dinner, the music of the orchestra floated up the elevator shaft to greet him. As he stepped into the thronged corridor, he sank back into one of the chairs against the wall to get his breath. The lights, the chatter, the perfumes, the bewildering medley of colour—he had, for a moment, the feeling of not being able to stand it. But only for a moment; these were his own people, he told himself. He went slowly about the corridors, through the writing-rooms, smoking-rooms, reception-rooms, as though he were exploring the chambers of an enchanted palace, built and peopled for him alone.

When he reached the dining-room he sat down at a table near a window. The flowers, the white linen, the many-coloured wine glasses, the gay toilettes of the women, the low popping of corks, the undulating repetitions of the *Blue Danube* from the orchestra, all flooded Paul's dream with bewildering radiance. When the roseate tinge of his champagne was added—that cold, precious, bubbling stuff that creamed and foamed in his glass—Paul wondered that there were honest men in the world at all. This was what all the world was fighting for, he reflected; this was what all the struggle was about. He doubted the reality of his past. Had he ever known a place called Cordelia Street, a place where fagged looking business men boarded the early car? Mere rivets in a machine they seemed to Paul,—sickening men, with combings of children's hair always hanging to their coats, and the smell of cooking in their clothes. Cordelia Street—Ah, that belonged to another time and country! Had he not always been thus, had he not sat here night after night, from as far back as he could remember, looking pensively over just such shimmering textures, and slowly twirling the stem of a glass like this one between his thumb and middle finger? He rather thought he had.

He was not in the least abashed or lonely. He had no especial desire to meet or to know any of these people; all he demanded was the right to look on and conjecture, to watch the pageant. The mere stage properties were all he contended for. Nor was he lonely later in the evening, in his loge at the Opera. He was entirely rid of his nervous misgivings, of his forced aggressiveness, of the imperative desire to show himself different from his surroundings. He felt now that his surroundings explained him. Nobody questioned the purple; he had only to wear it passively. He had only to glance down at his dress coat to reassure himself that here it would be impossible for anyone to humiliate him.

He found it hard to leave his beautiful sitting-room to go to bed that night, and sat long watching the raging storm from his turret window. When he went to sleep, it was with the lights turned on in his bedroom; partly because of his old timidity, and partly so that, if he should wake in the night, there would be no wretched moment of doubt, no horrible suspicion of yellow wall-paper, or of Washington and Calvin above his bed.

On Sunday morning the city was practically snow-bound. Paul breakfasted late, and in the afternoon he fell in with a wild San Francisco boy, a freshman at Yale, who said he had run down for a "little flyer" over Sunday. The young man offered to show Paul the night side of the town, and the two boys went off together after dinner, not returning to the hotel until seven o'clock the next morning. They had started out in the confiding warmth of a champagne friendship, but their parting in the elevator was singularly cool. The freshman pulled himself together to make his train, and Paul went to bed. He awoke at two o'clock in the afternoon, very thirsty and dizzy, and rang for ice-water, coffee, and the Pittsburgh papers.

On the part of the hotel management, Paul excited no suspicion. There was this to be said for him, that he wore his spoils with dignity and in no way made himself conspicuous. His chief greediness lay in his ears and eyes, and his excesses were not offensive ones. His dearest pleasures were the grey winter twilights in his sitting-room; his quiet enjoyment of his flowers, his clothes, his wide divan, his cigarette and his sense of power. He could not remember a time when he had felt so at peace with himself. The mere release from the necessity of petty lying, lying every day and every day, restored his self-respect. He had never lied for pleasure, even at school; but to make himself noticed and admired, to assert his difference from other Cordelia Street boys; and he felt a good deal more manly, more honest, even, now that he had no need for boastful pretensions, now that he could, as his actor friends used to say, "dress the part." It was characteristic that remorse did not occur to him. His golden days went by without a shadow, and he made each as perfect as he could.

On the eighth day after his arrival in New York, he found the whole affair exploited in the Pittsburgh papers, exploited with a wealth of detail which indicated that local news of a sensational nature was at a low ebb. The firm of Denny & Carson announced that the boy's father had refunded the full amount of his theft, and that they had no intention of prosecuting. The Cumberland minister had been interviewed, and expressed his hope of yet reclaiming the motherless lad, and Paul's Sabbath-school teacher declared that she would spare no effort to that end. The rumour had reached Pittsburgh that the boy had been seen in a New York hotel, and his father had gone East to find him and bring him home.

Paul had just come in to dress for dinner; he sank into a chair, weak in the knees, and clasped his head in his hands. It was to be worse than jail, even; the tepid waters of Cordelia Street were to close over him finally and forever. The grey monotony stretched before him in hopeless, unrelieved years; Sabbath-school, Young People's Meeting, the yellow-papered room, the damp dish-towels; it all rushed back upon him with sickening vividness. He had the old feeling that the orchestra had suddenly stopped, the sinking sensation that the play was over. The sweat broke out on his face, and he sprang to his feet, looked about him with his white, conscious smile, and winked at himself in the mirror. With something of the childish belief in miracles with which he had so often gone to class, all his lessons unlearned,

Paul dressed and dashed whistling down the corridor to the elevator.

He had no sooner entered the dining-room and caught the measure of the music, than his remembrance was lightened by his old elastic power of claiming the moment, mounting with it, and finding it all sufficient. The glare and glitter about him, the mere scenic accessories had again, and for the last time, their old potency. He would show himself that he was game, he would finish the thing splendidly. He doubted, more than ever, the existence of Cordelia Street, and for the first time he drank his wine recklessly. Was he not, after all, one of these fortunate beings? Was he not still himself, and in his own place? He drummed a nervous accompaniment to the music and looked about him, telling himself over and over that it had paid.

He reflected drowsily, to the swell of the violin and the chill sweetness of his wine, that he might have done it more wisely. He might have caught an outbound steamer and been well out of their clutches before now. But the other side of the world had seemed too far away and too uncertain then; he could not have waited for it; his need had been too sharp. If he had to choose over again, he would do the same thing tomorrow. He looked affectionately about the dining-room, now gilded with a soft mist. Ah, it had paid indeed!

Paul was awakened next morning by a painful throbbing in his head and feet. He had thrown himself across the bed without undressing, and had slept with his shoes on. His limbs and hands were lead heavy, and his tongue and throat were parched. There came upon him one of those fateful attacks of clear-headedness that never occurred except when he was physically exhausted and his nerves hung loose. He lay still and closed his eyes and let the tide of realities wash over him.

His father was in New York; "stopping at some joint or other," he told himself. The memory of successive summers on the front stoop fell upon him like a weight of black water. He had not a hundred dollars left; and he knew now, more than ever, that money was everything, the wall that stood between all he loathed and all he wanted. The thing was winding itself up; he had thought of that on his first glorious day in New York, and had even provided a way to snap the thread. It lay on his dressing-table now; he had got it out last night when he came blindly up from dinner,—but the shiny metal hurt his eyes, and he disliked the look of it, anyway.

He rose and moved about with a painful effort, succumbing now and again to attacks of nausea. It was the old depression exaggerated; all the world had become Cordelia Street. Yet somehow he was not afraid of anything, was absolutely calm; perhaps because he had looked into the dark corner at last, and knew. It was bad enough, what he saw there; but somehow not so bad as his long fear of it had been. He saw everything clearly now. He had a feeling that he had made the best of it, that he had lived the sort of life he was meant to live, and for half an hour he sat staring at the revolver. But he told himself that was not the way, so he went downstairs and took a cab to the ferry.

When Paul arrived at Newark, he got off the train and took another cab, directing the driver to follow the Pennsylvania tracks out of the town. The snow lay heavy on the roadways and had drifted deep in the open fields. Only here and there the dead grass or dried weed stalks projected, singularly black, above it. Once well into the country, Paul dismissed the carriage and walked, floundering along the tracks, his mind a medley of irrelevant things. He seemed to hold in his brain an actual picture of everything he had seen that morning. He remembered every feature of both his drivers, the toothless old woman from whom he had bought the red flowers in his coat, the agent from whom he had got his ticket, and all of his fellow-passengers on the ferry. His mind, unable to cope with vital matters near at hand, worked feverishly and deftly at sorting and grouping these images. They made for him a part of the ugliness of the world, of the ache in his head, and the bitter burning on his tongue. He stooped and put a handful of snow into his mouth as he walked, but that, too, seemed hot. When he reached a little hillside, where the tracks ran through a cut some twenty feet below him, he stopped and sat down.

The carnations in his coat were drooping with the cold, he noticed; all their red glory over. It occurred to him that all the flowers he had seen in the show windows that first night must have gone the same way, long before this. It was only one splendid breath they had, in spite of their brave mockery at the winter outside the glass. It was a losing game in the end, it seemed, this revolt against the homilies by which the world is run. Paul took one of the blossoms carefully from his coat and scooped a little hole in the snow, where he covered it up. Then he dozed a while, from his weak condition, seeming insensible to the cold.

The sound of an approaching train woke him, and he started to his feet, remembering only his resolution, and afraid lest he should be too late. He stood watching the approaching locomotive, his teeth chattering, his lips drawn away from them in a frightened smile; once or twice he glanced nervously sidewise, as though he were being watched. When the right moment came, he jumped. As he fell, the folly of his haste occurred to him with merciless clearness, the vastness of what he had left undone. There flashed through his brain, clearer than ever before, the blue of Adriatic water, the yellow of Algerian sands.

He felt something strike his chest,—his body was being thrown swiftly through the air, on and on, immeasurably far and fast, while his limbs gently relaxed. Then, because the picture making mechanism was crushed, the disturbing visions flashed into black, and Paul dropped back into the immense design of things.

A WAGNER MATINÉE

A WAGNER MATINÉE

I received one morning a letter, written in pale ink on glassy, blue-lined note-paper, and bearing the postmark of a little Nebraska village. This communication, worn and rubbed, looking as if it had been carried for some days in a coat pocket that was none too clean, was from my uncle Howard, and informed me that his wife had been left a small legacy by a bachelor relative, and that it would be necessary for her to go to Boston to attend to the settling of the estate. He requested me to meet her at the station and render her whatever services might be necessary. On examining the date indicated as that of her arrival, I found it to be no later than tomorrow. He had characteristically delayed writing until, had I been away from home for a day, I must have missed my aunt altogether.

The name of my Aunt Georgiana opened before me a gulf of recollection so wide and deep that, as the letter dropped from my hand, I felt suddenly a stranger to all the present conditions of my existence, wholly ill at ease and out of place amid the familiar surroundings of my study. I became, in short, the gangling farmer-boy my aunt had known, scourged with chilblains and bashfulness, my hands cracked and sore from the corn husking. I sat again before her parlour organ, fumbling the scales with my stiff, red fingers, while she, beside me, made canvas mittens for the huskers.

The next morning, after preparing my landlady for a visitor, I set out for the station. When the train arrived I had some difficulty in finding my aunt. She was the last of the passengers to alight, and it was not until I got her into the carriage that she seemed really to recognize me. She had come all the way in a day coach; her linen duster had become black with soot and her black bonnet grey with dust during the journey. When we arrived at my boarding-house the landlady put her to bed at once and I did not see her again until the next morning.

Whatever shock Mrs. Springer experienced at my aunt's appearance, she considerately concealed. As for myself, I saw my aunt's battered figure with that feeling of awe and respect with which we behold explorers who have left their ears and fingers north of Franz-Joseph-Land, or their health somewhere along the Upper Congo. My

Aunt Georgiana had been a music teacher at the Boston Conservatory, somewhere back in the latter sixties. One summer, while visiting in the little village among the Green Mountains where her ancestors had dwelt for generations, she had kindled the callow fancy of my uncle, Howard Carpenter, then an idle, shiftless boy of twenty-one. When she returned to her duties in Boston, Howard followed her, and the upshot of this infatuation was that she eloped with him, eluding the reproaches of her family and the criticism of her friends by going with him to the Nebraska frontier. Carpenter, who, of course, had no money, took up a homestead in Red Willow County, fifty miles from the railroad. There they had measured off their land themselves, driving across the prairie in a wagon, to the wheel of which they had tied a red cotton handkerchief, and counting its revolutions. They built a dug-out in the red hillside, one of those cave dwellings whose inmates so often reverted to primitive conditions. Their water they got from the lagoons where the buffalo drank, and their slender stock of provisions was always at the mercy of bands of roving Indians. For thirty years my aunt had not been farther than fifty miles from the homestead.

I owed to this woman most of the good that ever came my way in my boyhood, and had a reverential affection for her. During the years when I was riding herd for my uncle, my aunt, after cooking the three meals—the first of which was ready at six o'clock in the morning—and putting the six children to bed, would often stand until midnight at her ironing-board, with me at the kitchen table beside her, hearing me recite Latin declensions and conjugations, gently shaking me when my drowsy head sank down over a page of irregular verbs. It was to her, at her ironing or mending, that I read my first Shakspere, and her old text-book on mythology was the first that ever came into my empty hands. She taught me my scales and exercises on the little parlour organ which her husband had bought her after fifteen years during which she had not so much as seen a musical instrument. She would sit beside me by the hour, darning and counting, while I struggled with the "Joyous Farmer." She seldom talked to me about music, and I understood why. Once when I had been doggedly beating out some easy passages from an old score of *Euryanthe* I had found among her music books, she came up to me and, putting her hands over my eyes, gently drew my head back upon her shoulder, saying tremulously, "Don't love it so well, Clark, or it may be taken from you."

When my aunt appeared on the morning after her arrival in Boston, she was still in a semi-somnambulant state. She seemed not to realize that she was in the city where she had spent her youth, the place longed for hungrily half a lifetime. She had been so wretchedly train-sick throughout the journey that she had no recollection of anything but her discomfort, and, to all intents and purposes, there were but a few hours of nightmare between the farm in Red Willow County and my study on Newbury Street. I had planned a little pleasure for her that afternoon, to repay her for some of the glorious moments she had given me when we used to milk together in the straw-thatched cowshed and she, because I was more than usually tired, or because her husband had spoken sharply to me, would tell me of the splendid performance of the *Huguenots* she had seen in Paris, in her youth.

At two o'clock the Symphony Orchestra was to give a Wagner program, and I intended to take my aunt; though, as I conversed with her, I grew doubtful about her enjoyment of it. I suggested our visiting the Conservatory and the Common before lunch, but she seemed altogether too timid to wish to venture out. She questioned me absently about various changes in the city, but she was chiefly concerned that she had forgotten to leave instructions about feeding half-skimmed milk to a certain weakling calf, "old Maggie's calf, you know, Clark," she explained, evidently having forgotten how long I had been away. She was further troubled because she had neglected to tell her daughter about the freshly-opened kit of mackerel in the cellar, which would spoil if it were not used directly.

I asked her whether she had ever heard any of the Wagnerian operas, and found that she had not, though she was perfectly familiar with their respective situations, and had once possessed the piano score of *The Flying*

Dutchman. I began to think it would be best to get her back to Red Willow County without waking her, and regretted having suggested the concert.

From the time we entered the concert hall, however, she was a trifle less passive and inert, and for the first time seemed to perceive her surroundings. I had felt some trepidation lest she might become aware of her queer, country clothes, or might experience some painful embarrassment at stepping suddenly into the world to which she had been dead for a quarter of a century. But, again, I found how superficially I had judged her. She sat looking about her with eyes as impersonal, almost as stony, as those with which the granite Rameses in a museum watches the froth and fret that ebbs and flows about his pedestal. I have seen this same aloofness in old miners who drift into the Brown hotel at Denver, their pockets full of bullion, their linen soiled, their haggard faces unshaven; standing in the thronged corridors as solitary as though they were still in a frozen camp on the Yukon.

The matinée audience was made up chiefly of women. One lost the contour of faces and figures, indeed any effect of line whatever, and there was only the colour of bodices past counting, the shimmer of fabrics soft and firm, silky and sheer; red, mauve, pink, blue, lilac, purple, écru, rose, yellow, cream, and white, all the colours that an impressionist finds in a sunlit landscape, with here and there the dead shadow of a frock coat. My Aunt Georgiana regarded them as though they had been so many daubs of tube-paint on a palette.

When the musicians came out and took their places, she gave a little stir of anticipation, and looked with quickening interest down over the rail at that invariable grouping, perhaps the first wholly familiar thing that had greeted her eye since she had left old Maggie and her weakling calf. I could feel how all those details sank into her soul, for I had not forgotten how they had sunk into mine when I came fresh from ploughing forever and forever between green aisles of corn, where, as in a treadmill, one might walk from daybreak to dusk without perceiving a shadow of change. The clean profiles of the musicians, the gloss of their linen, the dull black of their coats, the beloved shapes of the instruments, the patches of yellow light on the smooth, varnished bellies of the 'cellos and the bass viols in the rear, the restless, wind-tossed forest of fiddle necks and bows— I recalled how, in the first orchestra I ever heard, those long bow-strokes seemed to draw the heart out of me, as a conjurer's stick reels out yards of paper ribbon from a hat.

The first number was the *Tannhäuser* overture. When the horns drew out the first strain of the Pilgrim's chorus, Aunt Georgiana clutched my coat sleeve. Then it was I first realized that for her this broke a silence of thirty years. With the battle between the two motives, with the frenzy of the Venusberg theme and its ripping of strings, there came to me an overwhelming sense of the waste and wear we are so powerless to combat; and I saw again the tall, naked house on the prairie, black and grim as a wooden fortress; the black pond where I had learned to swim, its margin pitted with sun-dried cattle tracks; the rain gullied clay banks about the naked house, the four dwarf ash seedlings where the dish-cloths were always hung to dry before the kitchen door. The world there was the flat world of the ancients; to the east, a cornfield that stretched to daybreak; to the west, a corral that reached to sunset; between, the conquests of peace, dearer-bought than those of war.

The overture closed, my aunt released my coat sleeve, but she said nothing. She sat staring dully at the orchestra. What, I wondered, did she get from it? She had been a good pianist in her day, I knew, and her musical education had been broader than that of most music teachers of a quarter of a century ago. She had often told me of Mozart's operas and Meyerbeer's, and I could remember hearing her sing, years ago, certain melodies of Verdi. When I had fallen ill with a fever in her house she used to sit by my cot in the evening—when the cool, night wind blew in through the faded mosquito netting tacked over the window and I lay watching a certain bright star that burned red above the cornfield—and sing "Home to our mountains, O, let us return!" in a way fit to break the heart of a Vermont boy near dead of homesickness already.

I watched her closely through the prelude to *Tristan and Isolde*, trying vainly to conjecture what that seething turmoil of strings and winds might mean to her, but she sat mutely staring at the violin bows that drove obliquely downward, like the pelting streaks of rain in a summer shower. Had this music any message for her? Had she enough left to at all comprehend this power which had kindled the world since she had left it? I was in a fever of curiosity, but Aunt Georgiana sat silent upon her peak in Darien. She preserved this utter immobility throughout the number from *The Flying Dutchman*, though her fingers worked mechanically upon her black dress, as if, of themselves, they were recalling the piano score they had once played. Poor hands! They had been stretched and twisted into mere tentacles to hold and lift and knead with;—on one of them a thin, worn band that had once been a wedding ring. As I pressed and gently quieted one of those groping hands, I remembered with quivering eyelids their services for me in other days.

Soon after the tenor began the "Prize Song," I heard a quick drawn breath and turned to my aunt. Her eyes were closed, but the tears were glistening on her cheeks, and I think, in a moment more, they were in my eyes as well. It never really died, then—the soul which can suffer so excruciatingly and so interminably; it withers to the outward eye only; like that strange moss which can lie on a dusty shelf half a century and yet, if placed in water, grows green again. She wept so throughout the development and elaboration of the melody.

During the intermission before the second half, I questioned my aunt and found that the "Prize Song" was not new to her. Some years before there had drifted to the farm in Red Willow County a young German, a tramp cow-puncher, who had sung in the chorus at Bayreuth when he was a boy, along with the other peasant boys and girls. Of a Sunday morning he used to sit on his gingham-sheeted bed in the hands' bedroom which opened off the kitchen, cleaning the leather of his boots and saddle, singing the "Prize Song," while my aunt went about her work in the kitchen. She had hovered over him until she had prevailed upon him to join the country church, though his sole fitness for this step, in so far as I could gather, lay in his boyish face and his possession of this divine melody. Shortly afterward, he had gone to town on the Fourth of July, been drunk for several days, lost his money at a faro table, ridden a saddled Texas steer on a bet, and disappeared with a fractured collar-bone. All this my aunt told me huskily, wanderingly, as though she were talking in the weak lapses of illness.

"Well, we have come to better things than the old *Trovatore* at any rate, Aunt Georgie?" I queried, with a well meant effort at jocularity.

Her lip quivered and she hastily put her handkerchief up to her mouth. From behind it she murmured, "And you have been hearing this ever since you left me,

Clark?" Her question was the gentlest and saddest of reproaches.

The second half of the program consisted of four numbers from the *Ring*, and closed with Siegfried's funeral march. My aunt wept quietly, but almost continuously, as a shallow vessel overflows in a rain-storm. From time to time her dim eyes looked up at the lights, burning softly under their dull glass globes.

The deluge of sound poured on and on; I never knew what she found in the shining current of it; I never knew how far it bore her, or past what happy islands. From the trembling of her face I could well believe that before the last number she had been carried out where the myriad graves are, into the grey, nameless burying grounds of the sea; or into some world of death vaster yet, where, from the beginning of the world, hope has lain down with hope and dream with dream and, renouncing, slept.

The concert was over; the people filed out of the hall chattering and laughing, glad to relax and find the living level again, but my kinswoman made no effort to rise. The harpist slipped the green felt cover over his instrument; the flute-players shook the water from their mouthpieces; the men of the orchestra went out one by one, leaving the stage to the chairs and music stands, empty as a winter cornfield.

I spoke to my aunt. She burst into tears and sobbed pleadingly. "I don't want to go, Clark, I don't want to go!"

I understood. For her, just outside the concert hall, lay the black pond with the cattle-tracked bluffs; the tall, unpainted house, with weather-curled boards, naked as a tower; the crook-backed ash seedlings where the dish-cloths hung to dry; the gaunt, moulting turkeys picking up refuse about the kitchen door.

THE SCULPTOR'S FUNERAL

THE SCULPTOR'S FUNERAL

A group of the townspeople stood on the station siding of a little Kansas town, awaiting the coming of the night train, which was already twenty minutes overdue. The snow had fallen thick over everything; in the pale starlight the line of bluffs across the wide, white meadows south of the town made soft, smoke-coloured curves against the clear sky. The men on the siding stood first on one foot and then on the other, their hands thrust deep into their trousers pockets, their overcoats open, their shoulders screwed up with the cold; and they glanced from time to time toward the southeast, where the railroad track wound along the river shore. They conversed in low tones and moved about restlessly, seeming uncertain as to what was expected of them. There was but one of the company who looked as if he knew exactly why he was there, and he kept conspicuously apart; walking to the far end of the platform, returning to the station door, then pacing up the track again, his chin sunk in the high collar of his overcoat, his burly shoulders drooping forward, his gait heavy and dogged. Presently he was approached by a tall, spare, grizzled man clad in a faded Grand Army suit, who shuffled out from the group and advanced with a certain deference, craning his neck forward until his back made the angle of a jack-knife three-quarters open.

"I reckon she's a-goin' to be pretty late agin tonight, Jim," he remarked in a squeaky falsetto. "S'pose it's the snow?"

"I don't know," responded the other man with a shade of annoyance, speaking from out an astonishing cataract of red beard that grew fiercely and thickly in all directions.

The spare man shifted the quill toothpick he was chewing to the other side of his mouth. "It ain't likely that anybody from the East will come with the corpse, I s'pose," he went on reflectively.

"I don't know," responded the other, more curtly than before.

"It's too bad he didn't belong to some lodge or other. I like an order funeral myself. They seem more appropriate for people of some repytation," the spare man continued, with an ingratiating concession in his shrill voice, as he carefully placed his toothpick in his vest pocket. He always carried the flag at the G.A.R. funerals in the town.

The heavy man turned on his heel, without replying, and walked up the siding. The spare man rejoined the uneasy group. "Jim's ez full ez a tick, ez ushel," he commented commiseratingly.

Just then a distant whistle sounded, and there was a shuffling of feet on the platform. A number of lanky boys, of all ages, appeared as suddenly and slimily as eels wakened by the crack of thunder; some came from the waiting-room, where they had been warming themselves by the red stove, or half asleep on the slat benches; others uncoiled themselves from baggage trucks or slid out of express wagons. Two clambered down from the driver's seat of a hearse that stood backed up against the siding. They straightened their stooping shoulders and lifted their heads, and a flash of momentary animation kindled their dull eyes at that cold, vibrant scream, the world-wide call for men. It stirred them like the note of a trumpet; just as it had often stirred the man who was coming home tonight, in his boyhood.

The night express shot, red as a rocket, from out the eastward marsh lands and wound along the river shore under the long lines of shivering poplars that sentinelled the meadows, the escaping steam hanging in grey masses against the pale sky and blotting out the Milky Way. In a moment the red glare from the headlight streamed up the snow-covered track before the siding and glittered on the wet, black rails. The burly man with the dishevelled red beard walked swiftly up the platform toward the approaching train, uncovering his head as he went. The group of men behind him hesitated, glanced questioningly at one another, and awkwardly followed his example. The train stopped, and the crowd shuffled up to the express car just as the door was thrown open, the man in the G.A.R. suit thrusting his head forward with curiosity. The express messenger appeared in the doorway, accompanied by a young man in a long ulster and travelling cap.

"Are Mr. Merrick's friends here?" inquired the young man.

The group on the platform swayed uneasily. Philip Phelps, the banker, responded with dignity: "We have come to take charge of the body. Mr. Merrick's father is very feeble and can't be about."

"Send the agent out here," growled the express messenger, "and tell the operator to lend a hand."

The coffin was got out of its rough-box and down on the snowy platform. The townspeople drew back enough to make room for it and then formed a close semicircle about it, looking curiously at the palm leaf which lay across the black cover. No one said anything. The baggage man stood by his truck, waiting to get at the trunks. The engine panted heavily, and the fireman dodged in and out among the wheels with his yellow torch and long oil-can, snapping the spindle boxes. The young Bostonian, one of the dead sculptor's pupils who had come with the body, looked about him helplessly. He turned to the banker, the only one of that black, uneasy, stoop-shouldered group who seemed enough of an individual to be addressed.

"None of Mr. Merrick's brothers are here?" he asked uncertainly.

The man with the red beard for the first time stepped up and joined the others. "No, they have not come yet; the family is scattered. The body will be taken directly to the house." He stooped and took hold of one of the handles of the coffin.

"Take the long hill road up, Thompson, it will be easier on the horses," called the liveryman as the under-taker snapped the door of the hearse and prepared to mount to the driver's seat.

Laird, the red-bearded lawyer, turned again to the stranger: "We didn't know whether there would be any one with him or not," he explained. "It's a long walk, so you'd better go up in the hack." He pointed to a single battered conveyance, but the young man replied stiffly: "Thank you, but I think I will go up with the hearse. If you don't object," turning to the undertaker, "I'll ride with you."

They clambered up over the wheels and drove off in the starlight up the long, white hill toward the town. The lamps in the still village were shining from under the low, snow-burdened roofs; and beyond, on every side, the plains reached out into emptiness, peaceful and wide as the soft sky itself, and wrapped in a tangible, white silence.

When the hearse backed up to a wooden sidewalk before a naked, weather-beaten frame house, the same composite, ill-defined group that had stood upon the station siding was huddled about the gate. The front yard was an icy swamp, and a couple of warped planks, extending from the sidewalk to the door, made a sort of rickety foot-bridge. The gate hung on one hinge, and was opened wide with difficulty. Steavens, the young stranger, noticed that something black was tied to the knob of the front door.

The grating sound made by the casket, as it was drawn from the hearse, was answered by a scream from the house; the front door was wrenched open, and a tall, corpulent woman rushed out bareheaded into the snow and flung herself upon the coffin, shrieking: "My boy, my boy! And this is how you've come home to me!"

As Steavens turned away and closed his eyes with a shudder of unutterable repulsion, another woman, also tall, but flat and angular, dressed entirely in black, darted out of the house and caught Mrs. Merrick by the shoulders, crying sharply: "Come, come, mother; you mustn't go on like this!" Her tone changed to one of obsequious solemnity as she turned to the banker: "The parlour is ready, Mr. Phelps."

The bearers carried the coffin along the narrow boards,

while the undertaker ran ahead with the coffin-rests. They bore it into a large, unheated room that smelled of dampness and disuse and furniture polish, and set it down under a hanging lamp ornamented with jingling glass prisms and before a "Rogers group" of John Alden and Priscilla, wreathed with smilax. Henry Steavens stared about him with the sickening conviction that there had been a mistake, and that he had somehow arrived at the wrong destination. He looked at the clover-green Brussels, the fat plush upholstery, among the hand-painted china placques and panels and vases, for some mark of identification, —for something that might once conceivably have belonged to Harvey Merrick. It was not until he recognized his friend in the crayon portrait of a little boy in kilts and curls, hanging above the piano, that he felt willing to let any of these people approach the coffin.

"Take the lid off, Mr. Thompson; let me see my boy's face," wailed the elder woman between her sobs. This time Steavens looked fearfully, almost beseechingly into her face, red and swollen under its masses of strong, black, shiny hair. He flushed, dropped his eyes, and then, almost incredulously, looked again. There was a kind of power about her face—a kind of brutal handsomeness, even; but it was scarred and furrowed by violence, and so coloured and coarsened by fiercer passions that grief seemed never to have laid a gentle finger there. The long nose was distended and knobbed at the end, and there were deep lines on either side of it; her heavy, black brows almost met across her forehead, her teeth were large and square, and set far apart—teeth that could tear. She filled the room; the men were obliterated, seemed tossed about like twigs in an angry water, and even Steavens felt himself being drawn into the whirlpool.

The daughter—the tall, raw-boned woman in crêpe, with a mourning comb in her hair which curiously lengthened her long face—sat stiffly upon the sofa, her hands, conspicuous for their large knuckles, folded in her lap, her mouth and eyes drawn down, solemnly awaiting the opening of the coffin. Near the door stood a mulatto woman, evidently a servant in the house, with a timid bearing and an emaciated face pitifully sad and gentle. She was weeping silently, the corner of her calico apron lifted to her eyes, occasionally suppressing a long, quivering sob. Steavens walked over and stood beside her.

Feeble steps were heard on the stairs, and an old man, tall and frail, odorous of pipe smoke, with shaggy, unkept grey hair and a dingy beard, tobacco stained about the mouth, entered uncertainly. He went slowly up to the coffin and stood rolling a blue cotton handkerchief between his hands, seeming so pained and embarrassed by his wife's orgy of grief that he had no consciousness of anything else.

"There, there, Annie, dear, don't take on so," he quavered timidly, putting out a shaking hand and awkwardly patting her elbow. She turned and sank upon his shoulder with such violence that he tottered a little.

He did not even glance toward the coffin, but continued to look at her with a dull, frightened, appealing expression, as a spaniel looks at the whip. His sunken cheeks slowly reddened and burned with miserable shame. When his wife rushed from the room, her daughter strode after her with set lips. The servant stole up to the coffin, bent over it for a moment, and then slipped away to the kitchen, leaving Steavens, the lawyer, and the father to themselves. The old man stood looking down at his dead son's face. The sculptor's splendid head seemed even more noble in its rigid stillness than in life. The dark hair had crept down upon the wide forehead; the face seemed strangely long, but in it there was not that repose we expect to find in the faces of the dead. The brows were so drawn that there were two deep lines above the beaked nose, and the chin was thrust forward defiantly. It was as though the strain of life had been so sharp and bitter that death could not at once relax the tension and smooth the countenance into perfect peace—as though he were still guarding something precious, which might even yet be wrested from him.

The old man's lips were working under his stained beard. He turned to the lawyer with timid deference: "Phelps and the rest are comin' back to set up with Harve, ain't they?" he asked. "Thank 'ee, Jim, thank 'ee." He brushed the hair back gently from his son's forehead. "He was a good boy, Jim; always a good boy. He was ez gentle ez a child and the kindest of 'em all—only we didn't none of us ever onderstand him." The tears trickled slowly down his beard and dropped upon the sculptor's coat.

"Martin, Martin! Oh, Martin! come here," his wife wailed from the top of the stairs. The old man started timorously: "Yes, Annie, I'm coming." He turned away, hesitated, stood for a moment in miserable indecision; then reached back and patted the dead man's hair softly, and stumbled from the room.

"Poor old man, I didn't think he had any tears left. Seems as if his eyes would have gone dry long ago. At his age nothing cuts very deep," remarked the lawyer.

Something in his tone made Steavens glance up. While the mother had been in the room, the young man had scarcely seen any one else; but now, from the moment he first glanced into Jim Laird's florid face and blood-shot eyes, he knew that he had found what he had been heartsick at not finding before—the feeling, the understanding, that must exist in some one, even here.

The man was red as his beard, with features swollen and blurred by dissipation, and a hot, blazing blue eye. His face was strained—that of a man who is controlling himself with difficulty—and he kept plucking at his beard with a sort of fierce resentment. Steavens, sitting by the window, watched him turn down the glaring lamp, still its jangling pendants with an angry gesture, and then stand with his hands locked behind him, staring down into the master's face. He could not help wondering what link there had been between the porcelain vessel and so sooty a lump of potter's clay.

From the kitchen an uproar was sounding; when the dining-room door opened, the import of it was clear. The mother was abusing the maid for having forgotten to make the dressing for the chicken salad which had been prepared for the watchers. Steavens had never heard anything in the least like it; it was injured, emotional, dramatic abuse, unique and masterly in its excruciating cruelty, as violent and unrestrained as had been her grief of twenty minutes before. With a shudder of disgust the lawyer went into the dining-room and closed the door into the kitchen.

"Poor Roxy's getting it now," he remarked when he came back. "The Merricks took her out of the poor-house years ago; and if her loyalty would let her, I guess the poor old thing could tell tales that would curdle your blood. She's the mulatto woman who was standing in here a while ago, with her apron to her eyes. The old woman is a fury; there never was anybody like her. She made Harvey's life a hell for him when he lived at home; he was so sick ashamed of it. I never could see how he kept himself sweet."

"He was wonderful," said Steavens slowly, "wonderful; but until tonight I have never known how wonderful."

"That is the eternal wonder of it, anyway; that it can come even from such a dung heap as this," the lawyer cried, with a sweeping gesture which seemed to indicate much more than the four walls within which they stood.

"I think I'll see whether I can get a little air. The room is so close I am beginning to feel rather faint," murmured Steavens, struggling with one of the windows. The sash was stuck, however, and would not yield, so he sat down dejectedly and began pulling at his collar. The lawyer came over, loosened the sash with one blow of his red fist and sent the window up a few inches. Steavens thanked him, but the nausea which had been gradually climbing into his throat for the last half hour left him with but one desire—a desperate feeling that he must get away from this place with what was left of Harvey Merrick. Oh, he comprehended well enough now the quiet bitterness of the smile that he had seen so often on his master's lips!

Once when Merrick returned from a visit home, he brought with him a singularly feeling and suggestive bas-relief of a thin, faded old woman, sitting and sewing something pinned to her knee; while a full-lipped, full-blooded little urchin, his trousers held up by a single gallows, stood beside her, impatiently twitching her gown to call her attention to a butterfly he had caught. Steavens, impressed by the tender and delicate modelling of the thin, tired face, had asked him if it were his mother. He remembered the dull flush that had burned up in the sculptor's face.

The lawyer was sitting in a rocking-chair beside the coffin, his head thrown back and his eyes closed. Steavens looked at him earnestly, puzzled at the line of the chin, and wondering why a man should conceal a feature of such distinction under that disfiguring shock of beard. Suddenly, as though he felt the young sculptor's keen glance, Jim Laird opened his eyes.

"Was he always a good deal of an oyster?" he asked abruptly. "He was terribly shy as a boy."

"Yes, he was an oyster, since you put it so," rejoined Steavens. "Although he could be very fond of people, he always gave one the impression of being detached. He disliked violent emotion; he was reflective, and rather distrustful of himself—except, of course, as regarded his work. He was sure enough there. He distrusted men pretty thoroughly and women even more, yet somehow without believing ill of them. He was determined, indeed, to believe the best; but he seemed afraid to investigate."

"A burnt dog dreads the fire," said the lawyer grimly, and closed his eyes.

Steavens went on and on, reconstructing that whole miserable boyhood. All this raw, biting ugliness had been the portion of the man whose mind was to become an exhaustless gallery of beautiful impressions—so sensitive that the mere shadow of a poplar leaf flickering against a sunny wall would be etched and held there for ever. Surely, if ever a man had the magic word in his finger tips, it was Merrick. Whatever he touched, he revealed its holiest secret; liberated it from enchantment and restored it to its pristine loveliness. Upon whatever

he had come in contact with, he had left a beautiful
record of the experience—a sort of ethereal signature; a
scent, a sound, a colour that was his own.

Steavens understood now the real tragedy of his master's life; neither love nor wine, as many had conjectured;
but a blow which had fallen earlier and cut deeper than
anything else could have done—a shame not his, and
yet so unescapably his, to hide in his heart from his very
boyhood. And without—the frontier warfare; the yearn-
ing of a boy, cast ashore upon a desert of newness and
ugliness and sordidness, for all that is chastened and old,
and noble with traditions.

At eleven o'clock the tall, flat woman in black announced that the watchers were arriving, and asked them
to "step into the dining-room." As Steavens rose, the
lawyer said dryly: "You go on—it'll be a good experience
for you. I'm not equal to that crowd tonight; I've had
twenty years of them."

As Steavens closed the door after him he glanced back
at the lawyer, sitting by the coffin in the dim light, with
his chin resting on his hand.

The same misty group that had stood before the door
of the express car shuffled into the dining-room. In the
light of the kerosene lamp they separated and became
individuals. The minister, a pale, feeble-looking man
with white hair and blond chin-whiskers, took his seat
beside a small side table and placed his Bible upon it.
The Grand Army man sat down behind the stove and

tilted his chair back comfortably against the wall, fishing his quill toothpick from his waistcoat pocket. The two bankers, Phelps and Elder, sat off in a corner behind the dinner-table, where they could finish their discussion of the new usury law and its effect on chattel security loans. The real estate agent, an old man with a smiling, hypocritical face, soon joined them. The coal and lumber dealer and the cattle shipper sat on opposite sides of the hard coal-burner, their feet on the nickel-work. Steavens took a book from his pocket and began to read. The talk around him ranged through various topics of local interest while the house was quieting down. When it was clear that the members of the family were in bed, the Grand Army man hitched his shoulders and, untangling his long legs, caught his heels on the rounds of his chair.

"S'pose there'll be a will, Phelps?" he queried in his weak falsetto.

The banker laughed disagreeably, and began trimming his nails with a pearl-handled pocket-knife.

"There'll scarcely be any need for one, will there?" he queried in his turn.

The restless Grand Army man shifted his position again, getting his knees still nearer his chin. "Why, the ole man says Harve's done right well lately," he chirped.

The other banker spoke up. "I reckon he means by that Harve ain't asked him to mortgage any more farms lately, so as he could go on with his education."

"Seems like my mind don't reach back to a time when

Harve wasn't bein' edycated," tittered the Grand Army man.

There was a general chuckle. The minister took out his handkerchief and blew his nose sonorously. Banker Phelps closed his knife with a snap. "It's too bad the old man's sons didn't turn out better," he remarked with reflective authority. "They never hung together. He spent money enough on Harve to stock a dozen cattle-farms, and he might as well have poured it into Sand Creek. If Harve had stayed at home and helped nurse what little they had, and gone into stock on the old man's bottom farm, they might all have been well fixed. But the old man had to trust everything to tenants and was cheated right and left."

"Harve never could have handled stock none," interposed the cattleman. "He hadn't it in him to be sharp. Do you remember when he bought Sander's mules for eight-year olds, when everybody in town knew that Sander's father-in-law give 'em to his wife for a wedding present eighteen years before, an' they was full-grown mules then?"

The company laughed discreetly, and the Grand Army man rubbed his knees with a spasm of childish delight.

"Harve never was much account for anything practical, and he shore was never fond of work," began the coal and lumber dealer. "I mind the last time he was home; the day he left, when the old man was out to the barn helpin' his hand hitch up to take Harve to the train, and

Cal Moots was patchin' up the fence; Harve, he come out on the step and sings out, in his ladylike voice: 'Cal Moots, Cal Moots! please come cord my trunk.' "

"That's Harve for you," approved the Grand Army man. "I kin hear him howlin' yet, when he was a big feller in long pants and his mother used to whale him with a rawhide in the barn for lettin' the cows git foundered in the cornfield when he was drivin' 'em home from pasture. He killed a cow of mine that-a-way onct— a pure Jersey and the best milker I had, an' the ole man had to put up for her. Harve, he was watchin' the sun set acrost the marshes when the anamile got away."

"Where the old man made his mistake was in sending the boy East to school," said Phelps, stroking his goatee and speaking in a deliberate, judicial tone. "There was where he got his head full of nonsense. What Harve needed, of all people, was a course in some first-class Kansas City business college."

The letters were swimming before Steavens's eyes. Was it possible that these men did not understand, that the palm on the coffin meant nothing to them? The very name of their town would have remained for ever buried in the postal guide had it not been now and again mentioned in the world in connection with Harvey Merrick's. He remembered what his master had said to him on the day of his death, after the congestion of both lungs had shut off any probability of recovery, and the sculptor had asked his pupil to send his body home. "It's not a pleasant place to be lying while the world is moving and doing and bettering," he had said with a feeble smile, "but it rather seems as though we ought to go back to the place we came from, in the end. The townspeople will come in for a look at me; and after they have had their say, I shan't have much to fear from the judgment of God!"

The cattleman took up the comment. "Forty's young for a Merrick to cash in; they usually hang on pretty well. Probably he helped it along with whisky."

"His mother's people were not long lived, and Harvey never had a robust constitution," said the minister mildly. He would have liked to say more. He had been the boy's Sunday-school teacher, and had been fond of him; but he felt that he was not in a position to speak. His own sons had turned out badly, and it was not a year since one of them had made his last trip home in the express car, shot in a gambling-house in the Black Hills.

"Nevertheless, there is no disputin' that Harve frequently looked upon the wine when it was red, also variegated, and it shore made an oncommon fool of him," moralized the cattleman.

Just then the door leading into the parlour rattled loudly and every one started involuntarily, looking relieved when only Jim Laird came out. The Grand Army man ducked his head when he saw the spark in his blue, blood-shot eye. They were all afraid of Jim; he was a drunkard, but he could twist the law to suit his client's needs as no other man in all western Kansas could do, and there were many who tried. The lawyer closed the door behind him, leaned back against it and folded his arms, cocking his head a little to one side. When he assumed this attitude in the court-room, ears were always pricked up, as it usually foretold a flood of withering sarcasm.

"I've been with you gentlemen before," he began in a dry, even tone, "when you've sat by the coffins of boys born and raised in this town; and, if I remember rightly, you were never any too well satisfied when you checked them up. What's the matter, anyhow? Why is it that reputable young men are as scarce as millionaires in Sand City? It might almost seem to a stranger that there was some way something the matter with your progressive town. Why did Ruben Sayer, the brightest young lawyer you ever turned out, after he had come home from the university as straight as a die, take to drinking and forge a check and shoot himself? Why did Bill Merrit's son die of the shakes in a saloon in Omaha? Why was Mr. Thomas's son, here, shot in a gambling-house? Why did young Adams burn his mill to beat the insurance companies and go to the pen?"

The lawyer paused and unfolded his arms, laying one clenched fist quietly on the table. "I'll tell you why. Because you drummed nothing but money and knavery into their ears from the time they wore knickerbockers; because you carped away at them as you've been carping here tonight, holding our friends Phelps and Elder up to them for their models, as our grandfathers held up George Washington and John Adams. But the boys were young, and raw at the business you put them to, and how could they match coppers with such artists as Phelps and Elder? You wanted them to be successful rascals; they were only unsuccessful ones—that's all the difference. There was only one boy ever raised in this borderland between ruffianism and civilization who didn't come to grief, and you hated Harvey Merrick more for winning out than you hated all the other boys who got under the wheels. Lord, Lord, how you did hate him! Phelps, here, is fond of saying that he could buy and sell us all out any time he's a mind to; but he knew Harve wouldn't have given a tinker's damn for his bank and all his cattlefarms put together; and a lack of appreciation, that way, goes hard with Phelps.

"Old Nimrod thinks Harve drank too much; and this from such as Nimrod and me!

"Brother Elder says Harve was too free with the old man's money—fell short in filial consideration, maybe. Well, we can all remember the very tone in which brother Elder swore his own father was a liar, in the county court; and we all know that the old man came out of that partnership with his son as bare as a sheared lamb. But maybe I'm getting personal, and I'd better be driving ahead at what I want to say."

The lawyer paused a moment, squared his heavy shoulders, and went on: "Harvey Merrick and I went to school together, back East. We were dead in earnest, and we wanted you all to be proud of us some day. We meant to be great men. Even I, and I haven't lost my sense of humour, gentlemen, I meant to be a great man. I came back here to practise, and I found you didn't in the least want me to be a great man. You wanted me to be a shrewd lawyer—oh, yes! Our veteran here wanted me to get him an increase of pension, because he had dyspepsia; Phelps wanted a new county survey that would put the widow Wilson's little bottom farm inside his south line; Elder wanted to lend money at 5 per cent. a month, and get it collected; and Stark here wanted to wheedle old women up in Vermont into investing their annuities in real-estate mortgages that are not worth the paper they are written on. Oh, you needed me hard enough, and you'll go on needing me!

"Well, I came back here and became the damned shyster you wanted me to be. You pretend to have some sort of respect for me; and yet you'll stand up and throw mud at Harvey Merrick, whose soul you couldn't dirty and whose hands you couldn't tie. Oh, you're a discriminating lot of Christians! There have been times when the sight of Harvey's name in some Eastern paper has made me hang my head like a whipped dog; and, again, times when I liked to think of him off there in the world, away from all this hog-wallow, climbing the big, clean upgrade he'd set for himself.

"And we? Now that we've fought and lied and sweated

and stolen, and hated as only the disappointed strugglers in a bitter, dead little Western town know how to do, what have we got to show for it? Harvey Merrick wouldn't have given one sunset over your marshes for all you've got put together, and you know it. It's not for me to say why, in the inscrutable wisdom of God, a genius should ever have been called from this place of hatred and bitter waters; but I want this Boston man to know that the drivel he's been hearing here tonight is the only tribute any truly great man could have from such a lot of sick, side-tracked, burnt-dog, land-poor sharks as the here-present financiers of Sand City—upon which town may God have mercy!"

The lawyer thrust out his hand to Steavens as he passed him, caught up his overcoat in the hall, and had left the house before the Grand Army man had had time to lift his ducked head and crane his long neck about at his fellows.

Next day Jim Laird was drunk and unable to attend the funeral services. Steavens called twice at his office, but was compelled to start East without seeing him. He had a presentiment that he would hear from him again, and left his address on the lawyer's table; but if Laird found it, he never acknowledged it. The thing in him that Harvey Merrick had loved must have gone under ground with Harvey Merrick's coffin; for it never spoke again, and Jim got the cold he died of driving across the Colorado mountains to defend one of Phelps's sons who had got into trouble out there by cutting government timber.

"A DEATH IN THE DESERT"

"A DEATH IN THE DESERT"

Everett Hilgarde was conscious that the man in the seat across the aisle was looking at him intently. He was a large, florid man, wore a conspicuous diamond solitaire upon his third finger, and Everett judged him to be a travelling salesman of some sort. He had the air of an adaptable fellow who had been about the world and who could keep cool and clean under almost any circumstances. The "High Line Flyer," as this train was derisively called among railroad men, was jerking along through the hot afternoon over the monotonous country between Holdredge and Cheyenne. Besides the blond man and himself the only occupants of the car were two dusty, bedraggled-looking girls who had been to the Exposition at Chicago, and who were earnestly discussing the cost of their first trip out of Colorado. The four uncomfortable passengers were covered with a sediment of fine, yellow dust which clung to their hair and eyebrows like gold powder. It blew up in clouds from the bleak, lifeless country through which they passed, until they were one colour with the sage-brush and sand-hills. The grey and yellow desert was varied only by occasional ruins of deserted towns, and the little red boxes of station-houses, where the spindling trees and sickly vines in the blue-grass yards made little green reserves fenced off in that confusing wilderness of sand.

As the slanting rays of the sun beat in stronger and stronger through the car-windows, the blond gentleman asked the ladies' permission to remove his coat, and sat in his lavender striped shirt-sleeves, with a black silk handkerchief tucked about his collar. He had seemed interested in Everett since they had boarded the train at Holdredge; kept glancing at him curiously and then looking reflectively out of the window, as though he were trying to recall something. But wherever Everett went, some one was almost sure to look at him with that curious interest, and it had ceased to embarrass or annoy him. Presently the stranger, seeming satisfied with his observation, leaned back in his seat, half closed his eyes, and began softly to whistle the Spring Song from *Proserpine*, the cantata that a dozen years before had made its young composer famous in a night. Everett had heard that air on guitars in Old Mexico, on mandolins at college glees, on cottage organs in New England hamlets, and only two weeks ago he had heard it played on sleigh bells at a variety theatre in Denver. There was literally no way of escaping his brother's precocity. Adriance could live on the other side of the Atlantic, where his youthful indiscretions were forgotten in his mature achievements, but his brother had never been able to outrun *Proserpine*,—and here he found it again, in the Colorado sand-hills. Not that Everett was exactly ashamed of *Proserpine;* only a man of genius could have written it, but it was the sort of thing that a man of genius outgrows as soon as he can.

Everett unbent a trifle, and smiled at his neighbour across the aisle. Immediately the large man rose and coming over dropped into the seat facing Hilgarde, extending his card.

"Dusty ride, isn't it? I don't mind it myself; I'm used to it. Born and bred in de briar patch, like Br'er Rabbit. I've been trying to place you for a long time; I think I must have met you before."

"Thank you," said Everett, taking the card; "my name is Hilgarde. You've probably met my brother, Adriance; people often mistake me for him."

The travelling-man brought his hand down upon his knee with such vehemence that the solitaire blazed.

"So I was right after all, and if you're not Adriance Hilgarde you're his double. I thought I couldn't be mistaken. Seen him? Well, I guess! I never missed one of his recitals at the Auditorium, and he played the piano score

of *Proserpine* through to us once at the Chicago Press
Club. I used to be on the *Commercial* there before I began to travel for the publishing department of the concern. So you're Hilgarde's brother, and here I've run
into you at the jumping-off place. Sounds like a newspaper yarn, doesn't it?"

The travelling-man laughed and offering Everett a
cigar plied him with questions on the only subject that
people ever seemed to care to talk to him about. At
length the salesman and the two girls alighted at a Colorado way station, and Everett went on to Cheyenne alone.

The train pulled into Cheyenne at nine o'clock, late
by a matter of four hours or so; but no one seemed
particularly concerned at its tardiness except the station
agent, who grumbled at being kept in the office over
time on a summer night. When Everett alighted from
the train he walked down the platform and stopped at
the track crossing, uncertain as to what direction he
should take to reach a hotel. A phaeton stood near the
crossing and a woman held the reins. She was dressed
in white, and her figure was clearly silhouetted against
the cushions, though it was too dark to see her face.
Everett had scarcely noticed her, when the switch-engine
came puffing up from the opposite direction, and the
head-light threw a strong glare of light on his face. The
woman in the phaeton uttered a low cry and dropped the
reins. Everett started forward and caught the horse's
head, but the animal only lifted its ears and whisked its

tail in impatient surprise. The woman sat perfectly still, her head sunk between her shoulders and her handkerchief pressed to her face. Another woman came out of the depot and hurried toward the phaeton, crying, "Katharine, dear, what is the matter?"

Everett hesitated a moment in painful embarrassment, then lifted his hat and passed on. He was accustomed to sudden recognitions in the most impossible places, especially from women.

While he was breakfasting the next morning, the head waiter leaned over his chair to murmur that there was a gentleman waiting to see him in the parlour. Everett finished his coffee, and went in the direction indicated, where he found his visitor restlessly pacing the floor. His whole manner betrayed a high degree of agitation, though his physique was not that of a man whose nerves lie near the surface. He was something below medium height, square-shouldered and solidly built. His thick, closely cut hair was beginning to show grey about the ears, and his bronzed face was heavily lined. His square brown hands were locked behind him, and he held his shoulders like a man conscious of responsibilities, yet, as he turned to greet Everett, there was an incongruous diffidence in his address.

"Good-morning, Mr. Hilgarde," he said, extending his hand; "I found your name on the hotel register. My name is Gaylord. I'm afraid my sister startled you at the station last night, and I've come around to explain."

"Ah! the young lady in the phaeton? I'm sure I didn't know whether I had anything to do with her alarm or not. If I did, it is I who owe an apology."

The man coloured a little under the dark brown of his face.

"Oh, it's nothing you could help, sir, I fully understand that. You see, my sister used to be a pupil of your brother's, and it seems you favour him; when the switch-engine threw a light on your face, it startled her."

Everett wheeled about in his chair. "Oh! *Katharine Gaylord*! Is it possible! Why, I used to know her when I was a boy. What on earth—"

"Is she doing here?" Gaylord grimly filled out the pause. "You've got at the heart of the matter. You know my sister had been in bad health for a long time?"

"No. The last I knew of her she was singing in London. My brother and I correspond infrequently, and seldom get beyond family matters. I am deeply sorry to hear this."

The lines in Charley Gaylord's brow relaxed a little.

"What I'm trying to say, Mr. Hilgarde, is that she wants to see you. She's set on it. We live several miles out of town, but my rig's below, and I can take you out any time you can go."

"At once, then. I'll get my hat and be with you in a moment."

When he came downstairs Everett found a cart at the door, and Charley Gaylord drew a long sigh of relief as he gathered up the reins and settled back into his own element.

"I think I'd better tell you something about my sister before you see her, and I don't know just where to begin. She travelled in Europe with your brother and his wife, and sang at a lot of his concerts; but I don't know just how much you know about her."

"Very little, except that my brother always thought her the most gifted of his pupils. When I knew her she was very young and very beautiful, and quite turned my head for a while."

Everett saw that Gaylord's mind was entirely taken up by his grief. "That's the whole thing," he went on, flecking his horses with the whip.

"She was a great woman, as you say, and she didn't come of a great family. She had to fight her own way from the first. She got to Chicago, and then to New York, and then to Europe, and got a taste for it all; and now she's dying here like a rat in a hole, out of her own world, and she can't fall back into ours. We've grown apart, some way—miles and miles apart—and I'm afraid she's fearfully unhappy."

"It's a tragic story you're telling me, Gaylord," said Everett. They were well out into the country now, spinning along over the dusty plains of red grass, with the ragged blue outline of the mountains before them.

"Tragic!" cried Gaylord, starting up in his seat, "my God, nobody will ever know how tragic! It's a tragedy I live with and eat with and sleep with, until I've lost my grip on everything. You see she had made a good bit of money, but she spent it all going to health resorts. It's her lungs. I've got money enough to send her anywhere, but the doctors all say it's no use. She hasn't the ghost of a chance. It's just getting through the days now. I had no notion she was half so bad before she came to me. She just wrote that she was run down. Now that she's here, I think she'd be happier anywhere under the sun, but she won't leave. She says it's easier to let go of life here. There was a time when I was a brakeman with a run out of Bird City, Iowa, and she was a little thing I could carry on my shoulder, when I could get her everything on earth she wanted, and she hadn't a wish my $80 a month didn't cover; and now, when I've got a little property together, I can't buy her a night's sleep!"

Everett saw that, whatever Charley Gaylord's present status in the world might be, he had brought the brakeman's heart up the ladder with him.

The reins slackened in Gaylord's hand as they drew up before a showily painted house with many gables and a round tower. "Here we are," he said, turning to Everett, "and I guess we understand each other."

They were met at the door by a thin, colourless woman, whom Gaylord introduced as "My sister, Maggie." She asked her brother to show Mr. Hilgarde into the music-room, where Katharine would join him.

When Everett entered the music-room he gave a little

start of surprise, feeling that he had stepped from the glaring Wyoming sunlight into some New York studio that he had always known. He looked incredulously out of the window at the grey plain that ended in the great upheaval of the Rockies.

The haunting air of familiarity perplexed him. Suddenly his eye fell upon a large photograph of his brother above the piano. Then it all became clear enough: this was veritably his brother's room. If it were not an exact copy of one of the many studios that Adriance had fitted up in various parts of the world, wearying of them and leaving almost before the renovator's varnish had dried, it was at least in the same tone. In every detail Adriance's taste was so manifest that the room seemed to exhale his personality.

Among the photographs on the wall there was one of Katharine Gaylord, taken in the days when Everett had known her, and when the flash of her eye or the flutter of her skirt was enough to set his boyish heart in a tumult. Even now, he stood before the portrait with a certain degree of embarrassment. It was the face of a woman already old in her first youth, a trifle hard, and it told of what her brother had called her fight. The *camaraderie* of her frank, confident eyes was qualified by the deep lines about her mouth and the curve of the lips, which was both sad and cynical. Certainly she had more good-will than confidence toward the world. The chief charm of the woman, as Everett had known her, lay in her superb figure and in her eyes, which possessed a warm, life-giving quality like the sunlight; eyes which glowed with a perpetual *salutat* to the world.

Everett was still standing before the picture, his hands behind him and his head inclined, when he heard the door open. A tall woman advanced toward him, holding out her hand. As she started to speak she coughed slightly, then, laughing, said, in a low, rich voice, a trifle husky: "You see I make the traditional Camille entrance. How good of you to come, Mr. Hilgarde."

Everett was acutely conscious that while addressing him she was not looking at him at all, and, as he assured her of his pleasure in coming, he was glad to have an opportunity to collect himself. He had not reckoned upon the ravages of a long illness. The long, loose folds of her white gown had been especially designed to conceal the sharp outlines of her body, but the stamp of her disease was there; simple and ugly and obtrusive, a pitiless fact that could not be disguised or evaded. The splendid shoulders were stooped, there was a swaying unevenness in her gait, her arms seemed disproportionately long, and her hands were transparently white, and cold to the touch. The changes in her face were less obvious; the proud carriage of the head, the warm, clear eyes, even the delicate flush of colour in her cheeks, all defiantly remained, though they were all in a lower key—older, sadder, softer.

She sat down upon the divan and began nervously to

arrange the pillows. "Of course I'm ill, and I look it, but you must be quite frank and sensible about that and get used to it at once, for we've no time to lose. And if I'm a trifle irritable you won't mind?—for I'm more than usually nervous."

"Don't bother with me this morning, if you are tired," urged Everett. "I can come quite as well tomorrow."

"Gracious, no!" she protested, with a flash of that quick, keen humour that he remembered as a part of her. "It's solitude that I'm tired to death of—solitude and the wrong kind of people. You see, the minister called on me this morning. He happened to be riding by on his bicycle and felt it his duty to stop. The funniest feature of his conversation is that he is always excusing my own profession to me. But how we are losing time! Do tell me about New York; Charley says you're just on from there. How does it look and taste and smell just now? I think a whiff of the Jersey ferry would be as flagons of cod-liver oil to me. Are the trees still green in Madison Square, or have they grown brown and dusty? Does the chaste Diana still keep her vows through all the exasperating changes of weather? Who has your brother's old studio now, and what misguided aspirants practise their scales in the rookeries about Carnegie Hall? What do people go to see at the theatres, and what do they eat and drink in the world nowadays? Oh, let me die in Harlem!" she was interrupted by a violent attack of coughing, and Everett, embarrassed by her discomfort, plunged into gossip about the professional people he had met in town during the summer, and the musical outlook for the winter. He was diagramming with his pencil some new mechanical device to be used at the Metropolitan in the production of the *Rheingold*, when he became conscious that she was looking at him intently, and that he was talking to the four walls.

Katharine was lying back among the pillows, watching him through half-closed eyes, as a painter looks at a picture. He finished his explanation vaguely enough and put the pencil back in his pocket. As he did so, she said, quietly: "How wonderfully like Adriance you are!"

He laughed, looking up at her with a touch of pride in his eyes that made them seem quite boyish. "Yes, isn't it absurd? It's almost as awkward as looking like Napoleon— But, after all, there are some advantages. It has made some of his friends like me, and I hope it will make you."

Katharine gave him a quick, meaning glance from under her lashes. "Oh, it did that long ago. What a haughty, reserved youth you were then, and how you used to stare at people, and then blush and look cross. Do you remember that night you took me home from a rehearsal, and scarcely spoke a word to me?"

"It was the silence of admiration," protested Everett, "very crude and boyish, but certainly sincere. Perhaps you suspected something of the sort?"

"I believe I suspected a pose; the one that boys often

affect with singers. But it rather surprised me in you, for you must have seen a good deal of your brother's pupils." Everett shook his head. "I saw my brother's pupils come and go. Sometimes I was called on to play accompaniments, or to fill out a vacancy at a rehearsal, or to order a carriage for an infuriated soprano who had thrown up her part. But they never spent any time on me, unless it was to notice the resemblance you speak of."

"Yes," observed Katharine, thoughtfully, "I noticed it then, too; but it has grown as you have grown older. That is rather strange, when you have lived such different lives. It's not merely an ordinary family likeness of features, you know, but the suggestion of the other man's personality in your face—like an air transposed to another key. But I'm not attempting to define it; it's beyond me; something altogether unusual and a trifle—well, uncanny," she finished, laughing.

Everett sat looking out under the red window-blind which was raised just a little. As it swung back and forth in the wind it revealed the glaring panorama of the desert —a blinding stretch of yellow, flat as the sea in dead calm, splotched here and there with deep purple shadows; and, beyond, the ragged blue outline of the mountains and the peaks of snow, white as the white clouds. "I remember, when I was a child I used to be very sensitive about it. I don't think it exactly displeased me, or that I would have had it otherwise, but it seemed like a birthmark, or something not to be lightly spoken of. It came

into even my relations with my mother. Ad went abroad
to study when he was very young, and mother was all
broken up over it. She did her whole duty by each of us,
but it was generally understood among us that she'd
have made burnt-offerings of us all for him any day. I
was a little fellow then, and when she sat alone on the
porch on summer evenings, she used sometimes to call
me to her and turn my face up in the light that streamed
out through the shutters and kiss me, and then I always
knew she was thinking of Adriance."

"Poor little chap," said Katharine, in her husky voice.
"How fond people have always been of Adriance! Tell
me the latest news of him. I haven't heard, except through
the press, for a year or more. He was in Algiers then, in
the valley of the Chelif, riding horseback, and he had
quite made up his mind to adopt the Mahometan faith
and become an Arab. How many countries and faiths
has he adopted, I wonder?"

"Oh, that's Adriance," chuckled Everett. "He is himself barely long enough to write checks and be measured
for his clothes. I didn't hear from him while he was an
Arab; I missed that."

"He was writing an Algerian *suite* for the piano then;
it must be in the publisher's hands by this time. I have
been too ill to answer his letter, and have lost touch
with him."

Everett drew an envelope from his pocket. "This came
a month ago. Read it at your leisure."

"Thanks. I shall keep it as a hostage. Now I want you to play for me. Whatever you like; but if there is anything new in the world, in mercy let me hear it."

He sat down at the piano, and Katharine sat near him, absorbed in his remarkable physical likeness to his brother, and trying to discover in just what it consisted. He was of a larger build than Adriance, and much heavier. His face was of the same oval mould, but it was grey, and darkened about the mouth by continual shaving. His eyes were of the same inconstant April colour, but they were reflective and rather dull; while Adriance's were always points of high light, and always meaning another thing than the thing they meant yesterday. It was hard to see why this earnest man should so continually suggest that lyric, youthful face, as gay as his was grave. For Adriance, though he was ten years the elder, and though his hair was streaked with silver, had the face of a boy of twenty, so mobile that it told his thoughts before he could put them into words. A contralto, famous for the extravagance of her vocal methods and of her affections, once said that the shepherd-boys who sang in the Vale of Tempe must certainly have looked like young Hilgarde.

Everett sat smoking on the veranda of the Inter-Ocean House that night, the victim of mournful recollections. His infatuation for Katharine Gaylord, visionary as it was, had been the most serious of his boyish love-affairs.

The fact that it was all so done and dead and far behind him, and that the woman had lived her life out since then, gave him an oppressive sense of age and loss.

He remembered how bitter and morose he had grown during his stay at his brother's studio when Katharine Gaylord was working there, and how he had wounded Adriance on the night of his last concert in New York. He had sat there in the box—while his brother and Katharine were called back again and again, and the flowers went up over the footlights until they were stacked half as high as the piano—brooding in his sullen boy's heart upon the pride those two felt in each other's work—spurring each other to their best and beautifully contending in song. The footlights had seemed a hard, glittering line drawn sharply between their life and his. He walked back to his hotel alone, and sat in his window staring out on Madison Square until long after midnight, resolved to beat no more at doors that he could never enter.

Everett's week in Cheyenne stretched to three, and he saw no prospect of release except through the thing he dreaded. The bright, windy days of the Wyoming autumn passed swiftly. Letters and telegrams came urging him to hasten his trip to the coast, but he resolutely postponed his business engagements. The mornings he spent on one of Charley Gaylord's ponies, or fishing in the mountains. In the afternoon he was usually at his post of duty.

Destiny, he reflected, seems to have very positive notions about the sort of parts we are fitted to play. The scene changes and the compensation varies, but in the end we usually find that we have played the same class of business from first to last. Everett had been a stop-gap all his life. He remembered going through a looking-glass labyrinth when he was a boy, and trying gallery after gallery, only at every turn to bump his nose against his own face—which, indeed, was not his own, but his brother's. No matter what his mission, east or west, by land or sea, he was sure to find himself employed in his brother's business, one of the tributary lives which helped to swell the shining current of Adriance Hilgarde's. It was not the first time that his duty had been to comfort, as best he could, one of the broken things his brother's imperious speed had cast aside and forgotten. He made no attempt to analyse the situation or to state it in exact terms; but he accepted it as a commission from his brother to help this woman to die. Day by day he felt her need for him grow more acute and positive; and day by day he felt that in his peculiar relation to her, his own individuality played a smaller part. His power to minister to her comfort lay solely in his link with his brother's life. He knew that she sat by him always watching for some trick of gesture, some familiar play of expression, some illusion of light and shadow, in which he should seem wholly Adriance. He knew that she lived upon this, and that in the exhaustion which followed this turmoil of her dying senses, she slept deep and sweet, and dreamed of youth and art and days in a certain old Florentine garden, and not of bitterness and death.

A few days after his first meeting with Katharine Gaylord, he had cabled his brother to write her. He merely said that she was mortally ill; he could depend on Adriance to say the right thing—that was a part of his gift. Adriance always said not only the right thing, but the opportune, graceful, exquisite thing. He caught the lyric essence of the moment, the poetic suggestion of every situation. Moreover, he usually did the right thing,— except, when he did very cruel things—bent upon making people happy when their existence touched his, just as he insisted that his material environment should be beautiful; lavishing upon those near him all the warmth and radiance of his rich nature, all the homage of the poet and troubadour, and, when they were no longer near, forgetting—for that also was a part of Adriance's gift.

Three weeks after Everett had sent his cable, when he made his daily call at the gaily painted ranch-house, he found Katharine laughing like a girl. "Have you ever thought," she said, as he entered the music-room, "how much these séances of ours are like Heine's 'Florentine Nights,' except that I don't give you an opportunity to monopolize the conversation?" She held his hand longer than usual as she greeted him. "You are the kindest man living, the kindest," she added, softly.

Everett's grey face coloured faintly as he drew his

hand away, for he felt that this time she was looking at him, and not at a whimsical caricature of his brother.

She drew a letter with a foreign postmark from between the leaves of a book and held it out, smiling. "You got him to write it. Don't say you didn't, for it came direct, you see, and the last address I gave him was a place in Florida. This deed shall be remembered of you when I am with the just in Paradise. But one thing you did not ask him to do, for you didn't know about it. He has sent me his latest work, the new sonata, and you are to play it for me directly. But first for the letter; I think you would better read it aloud to me."

Everett sat down in a low chair facing the window-seat in which she reclined with a barricade of pillows behind her. He opened the letter, his lashes half-veiling his kind eyes, and saw to his satisfaction that it was a long one; wonderfully tactful and tender, even for Adriance, who was tender with his valet and his stable-boy, with his old gondolier and the beggar-women who prayed to the saints for him.

The letter was from Granada, written in the Alhambra, as he sat by the fountain of the Patio di Lindaraxa. The air was heavy with the warm fragrance of the South and full of the sound of splashing, running water, as it had been in a certain old garden in Florence, long ago. The sky was one great turquoise, heated until it glowed. The wonderful Moorish arches threw graceful blue shadows all about him. He had sketched an outline of them on the margin of his note-paper. The letter was full of confidences about his work, and delicate allusions to their old happy days of study and comradeship.

As Everett folded it he felt that Adriance had divined the thing needed and had risen to it in his own wonderful way. The letter was consistently egotistical, and seemed to him even a trifle patronizing, yet it was just what she had wanted. A strong realization of his brother's charm and intensity and power came over him; he felt the breath of that whirlwind of flame in which Adriance passed, consuming all in his path, and himself even more resolutely than he consumed others. Then he looked down at this white, burnt-out brand that lay before him.

"Like him, isn't it?" she said, quietly. "I think I can scarcely answer his letter, but when you see him next you can do that for me. I want you to tell him many things for me, yet they can all be summed up in this: I want him to grow wholly into his best and greatest self, even at the cost of what is half his charm to you and me. Do you understand me?"

"I know perfectly well what you mean," answered Everett, thoughtfully. "And yet it's difficult to prescribe for those fellows; so little makes, so little mars."

Katharine raised herself upon her elbow, and her face flushed with feverish earnestness. "Ah, but it is the waste of himself that I mean; his lashing himself out on stupid and uncomprehending people until they take him at their own estimate."

"Come, come," expostulated Everett, now alarmed at her excitement. "Where is the new sonata? Let him speak for himself."

He sat down at the piano and began playing the first movement, which was indeed the voice of Adriance, his proper speech. The sonata was the most ambitious work he had done up to that time, and marked the transition from his early lyric vein to a deeper and nobler style. Everett played intelligently and with that sympathetic comprehension which seems peculiar to a certain lovable class of men who never accomplish anything in particular. When he had finished he turned to Katharine.

"How he has grown!" she cried. "What the three last years have done for him! He used to write only the tragedies of passion; but this is the tragedy of effort and failure, the thing Keats called hell. This is my tragedy, as I lie here, listening to the feet of the runners as they pass me—ah, God! the swift feet of the runners!"

She turned her face away and covered it with her hands. Everett crossed over to her and knelt beside her. In all the days he had known her she had never before, beyond an occasional ironical jest, given voice to the bitterness of her own defeat. Her courage had become a point of pride with him.

"Don't do it," he gasped. "I can't stand it, I really can't, I feel it too much."

When she turned her face back to him there was a ghost of the old, brave, cynical smile on it, more bitter than the tears she could not shed. "No, I won't; I will save that for the night, when I have no better company. Run over that theme at the beginning again, will you? It was running in his head when we were in Venice years ago, and he used to drum it on his glass at the dinner-table. He had just begun to work it out when the late autumn came on, and he decided to go to Florence for the winter. He lost touch with his idea, I suppose, during his illness. Do you remember those frightful days? All the people who have loved him are not strong enough to save him from himself! When I got word from Florence that he had been ill, I was singing at Monte Carlo. His wife was hurrying to him from Paris, but I reached him first. I arrived at dusk, in a terrific storm. They had taken an old palace there for the winter, and I found him in the library—a long, dark room full of old Latin books and heavy furniture and bronzes. He was sitting by a wood fire at one end of the room, looking, oh, so worn and pale!—as he always does when he is ill, you know. Ah, it is so good that you *do* know! Even his red smoking-jacket lent no colour to his face. His first words were not to tell me how ill he had been, but that that morning he had been well enough to put the last strokes to the score of his 'Souvenirs d'Automne,' and he was as I most like to remember him; calm and happy, and tired with that heavenly tiredness that comes after a good work done at last. Outside, the rain poured down in torrents, and the wind moaned and sobbed in the garden and about the walls of that desolated old palace. How that night comes back to me! There were no lights in the room, only the wood fire. It glowed on the black walls and floor like the reflection of purgatorial flame. Beyond us it scarcely penetrated the gloom at all. Adriance sat staring at the fire with the weariness of all his life in his eyes, and of all the other lives that must aspire and suffer to make up one such life as his. Somehow the wind with all its world-pain had got into the room, and the cold rain was in our eyes, and the wave came up in both of us at once—that awful vague, universal pain, that cold fear of life and death and God and hope—and we were like two clinging together on a spar in mid-ocean after the shipwreck of everything. Then we heard the front door open with a great gust of wind that shook even the walls, and the servants came running with lights, announcing that Madame had returned, '*and in the book we read no more than night.*' "

She gave the old line with a certain bitter humour, and with the hard, bright smile in which of old she had wrapped her weakness as in a glittering garment. That ironical smile, worn through so many years, had gradually changed the lines of her face, and when she looked in the mirror she saw not herself, but the scathing critic, the amused observer and satirist of herself.

Everett dropped his head upon his hand. "How much you have cared!" he said.

"Ah, yes, I cared," she replied, closing her eyes.

"You can't imagine what a comfort it is to have you know how I cared, what a relief it is to be able to tell it to some one."

Everett continued to look helplessly at the floor. "I was not sure how much you wanted me to know," he said.

"Oh, I intended you should know from the first time I looked into your face, when you came that day with Charley. You are so like him, that it is almost like telling him himself. At least, I feel now that he will know some day, and then I will be quite sacred from his compassion."

"And has he never known at all?" asked Everett, in a thick voice.

"Oh! never at all in the way that you mean. Of course, he is accustomed to looking into the eyes of women and finding love there; when he doesn't find it there he thinks he must have been guilty of some discourtesy. He has a genuine fondness for every woman who is not stupid or gloomy, or old or preternaturally ugly. I shared with the rest; shared the smiles and the gallantries and the droll little sermons. It was quite like a Sunday-school picnic; we wore our best clothes and a smile and took our turns. It was his kindness that was hardest."

"Don't; you'll make me hate him," groaned Everett.

Katharine laughed and began to play nervously with her fan. "It wasn't in the slightest degree his fault; that is the most grotesque part of it. Why, it had really begun before I ever met him. I fought my way to him, and I drank my doom greedily enough."

Everett rose and stood hesitating. "I think I must go. You ought to be quiet, and I don't think I can hear any more just now."

She put out her hand and took his playfully. "You've put in three weeks at this sort of thing, haven't you? Well, it ought to square accounts for a much worse life than yours will ever be."

He knelt beside her, saying, brokenly: "I stayed because I wanted to be with you, that's all. I have never cared about other women since I knew you in New York when I was a lad. You are a part of my destiny, and I could not leave you if I would."

She put her hands on his shoulders and shook her head. "No, no; don't tell me that. I have seen enough tragedy. It was only a boy's fancy, and your divine pity and my utter pitiableness have recalled it for a moment. One does not love the dying, dear friend. Now go, and you will come again tomorrow, as long as there are tomorrows." She took his hand with a smile that was both courage and despair, and full of infinite loyalty and tenderness, as she said softly:

> *"For ever and for ever, farewell, Cassius;*
> *If we do meet again, why, we shall smile;*
> *If not, why then, this parting was well made."*

The courage in her eyes was like the clear light of a star to him as he went out.

On the night of Adriance Hilgarde's opening concert

in Paris, Everett sat by the bed in the ranch-house in Wyoming, watching over the last battle that we have with the flesh before we are done with it and free of it for ever. At times it seemed that the serene soul of her must have left already and found some refuge from the storm, and only the tenacious animal life were left to do battle with death. She laboured under a delusion at once pitiful and merciful, thinking that she was in the Pullman on her way to New York, going back to her life and her work. When she roused from her stupor, it was only to ask the porter to waken her half an hour out of Jersey City, or to remonstrate about the delays and the roughness of the road. At midnight Everett and the nurse were left alone with her. Poor Charley Gaylord had lain down on a couch outside the door. Everett sat looking at the sputtering night-lamp until it made his eyes ache. His head dropped forward, and he sank into heavy, distressful slumber. He was dreaming of Adriance's concert in Paris, and of Adriance, the troubadour. He heard the applause and he saw the flowers going up over the footlights until they were stacked half as high as the piano, and the petals fell and scattered, making crimson splotches on the floor. Down this crimson pathway came Adriance with his youthful step, leading his singer by the hand; a dark woman this time, with Spanish eyes.

The nurse touched him on the shoulder, he started and awoke. She screened the lamp with her hand. Everett saw that Katharine was awake and conscious, and struggling a little. He lifted her gently on his arm and began to fan her. She looked into his face with eyes that seemed never to have wept or doubted. "Ah, dear Adriance, dear, dear!" she whispered.

Everett went to call her brother, but when they came back the madness of art was over for Katharine.

Two days later Everett was pacing the station siding, waiting for the west-bound train. Charley Gaylord walked beside him, but the two men had nothing to say to each other. Everett's bags were piled on the truck, and his step was hurried and his eyes were full of impatience, as he gazed again and again up the track, watching for the train. Gaylord's impatience was not less than his own; these two, who had grown so close, had now become painful and impossible to each other, and longed for the wrench of farewell.

As the train pulled in, Everett wrung Gaylord's hand among the crowd of alighting passengers. The people of a German opera company, *en route* for the coast, rushed by them in frantic haste to snatch their breakfast during the stop. Everett heard an exclamation, and a stout woman rushed up to him, glowing with joyful surprise and caught his coat-sleeve with her tightly gloved hands.

"*Herr Gott*, Adriance, *lieber Freund*," she cried.

Everett lifted his hat, blushing. "Pardon me, madame. I see that you have mistaken me for Adriance Hilgarde. I am his brother." Turning from the crestfallen singer he hurried into the car.

ABOUT THE AUTHOR

WILLA CATHER (1873–1947) was born near Winchester, Virginia. When she was ten, her family moved from the peace of Virginia to the wild prairies of Nebraska. She was graduated from the University of Nebraska at twenty-one, and did newspaper work and teaching in Pittsburgh, Pennsylvania, for the next few years. She published a book of verse, *April Twilights*, in 1903, and a book of short stories, *The Troll Garden*, in 1905. They were followed, over the years, by twelve novels, including *Death Comes for the Archbishop* and *Shadows on the Rock* (both are available in Vintage Books); four volumes of short stories, and two volumes of essays. Willa Cather was awarded the Pulitzer Prize for fiction in 1923.